Anticipation shot from her lips all the way down to her toes. She swallowed. "Just one kiss?"

"Only one," he whispered.

Slowly, as if giving her the chance to say no or back away again, he brought his mouth toward hers.

Every nerve ending tingled in hope. But a voice—common sense, perhaps?—shouted a warning.

Too late. She raised her chin and closed her eyes.

His lips touched gently against hers, as if joining something delicate or fragile. Light, soft, tender.

The way he kissed made her feel cherished and adored, and she liked thinking he cared for her in that way. An inviting warmth, like a sunny day after a rainstorm, settled over her, making her feel as if she'd finally reached the destination she'd been seeking.

Drake kept his hands at his sides and only touched her with his lips. Yet she felt a closeness, as if she were being embraced.

Not at all how she'd thought Drake Llewelyn would kiss, but it was enough to tell her what she'd known in her heart, what she'd feared.

One kiss would never be enough.

Dear Reader,

Harlequin books have been part of my life since my senior year of high school. I was sitting in English class and our teacher, Mrs. Cooper, told us we'd be studying different types of writing. One of my classmates arrived with a brown paper grocery sack filled with Harlequin® Romance novels that belonged to her mother. The books were passed out to each of us to read. A writing assignment would follow.

I had no idea what to expect, since I'd never read a Harlequin romance. But the exotic setting—the Canary Islands—and the relationship between the hero and heroine swept me away. I turned in my assignment, but I wanted to read more. The stories transported me far away from my studies. I could lose myself in the pages, where I could fall in love and know a happy ending was guaranteed. Talk about the perfect escape!

After graduation, I remember sitting on my futon in my apartment in Tempe, Arizona. I had just finished a Harlequin Romance novel. I imagined my name on the cover. I wondered if I could write one myself, if I had what it takes to make a reader's heart go "awww," the way mine did when I read the books. I decided to take the plunge.

I quickly learned that it's easier to read a romance than to write one for publication. But I persevered, and was thrilled when, in 1999, my first romance was published by Silhouette Yours Truly. Now my name is on the cover of Harlequin Romance novels, just as I had dreamed.

So here's to dreams coming true…the promise of Harlequin Romance! While *The Billionaire's Proposal* is very different from that first romance I read all those years ago, the exotic locations and that promise of a happy ending are the same. I hope you enjoy reading about Chaney and Drake as they tumble heart first into a relationship neither wanted, and find their dreams come true!

Happy sixtieth birthday, Harlequin!

Melissa

MELISSA McCLONE

Memo: The Billionaire's Proposal

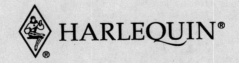

TORONTO • NEW YORK • LONDON
AMSTERDAM • PARIS • SYDNEY • HAMBURG
STOCKHOLM • ATHENS • TOKYO • MILAN • MADRID
PRAGUE • WARSAW • BUDAPEST • AUCKLAND

Recycling programs
for this product may
not exist in your area.

ISBN-13: 978-0-373-18466-8

MEMO: THE BILLIONAIRE'S PROPOSAL

First North American Publication 2009.

Copyright © 2009 by Melissa Martinez McClone.

www.eHarlequin.com

Printed in U.S.A.

With a degree in mechanical engineering from Stanford University, the last thing **Melissa McClone** ever thought she would be doing was writing romance novels. But analyzing engines for a major U.S. airline just couldn't compete with her happily-ever-afters. When she isn't writing, caring for her three young children or doing laundry, Melissa loves to curl up on the couch with a cup of tea, her cats and a good book. She also enjoys watching home-decorating shows to get ideas for her house—a 1939 cottage that is *slowly* being renovated. Melissa lives in Lake Oswego, Oregon, with her own real-life-hero husband, two daughters, a son, two lovable but oh-so-spoiled indoor cats, and a no-longer-stray outdoor kitty that decided to call the garage home. Melissa loves to hear from her readers. You can write to her at P.O. Box 63, Lake Oswego, OR 97034, U.S.A., or contact her via her Web site, www.melissamcclone.com.

For my blog readers, especially Amy,
Brandy, catslady, Dru, Jane, limecello, Nathalie,
Rottie_mom, Sarita, Tori and Virginia,
whose daily comments kept me smiling
while I finished writing this book.

Special thanks to Robin Barrett, M.D.,
Roxanne and Brian Coyne, Greg Taylor,
Virginia Kantra, Terri Reed and my family.

PROLOGUE

"I KNEW this internship was a chance of a lifetime, but I never thought I'd make so many wonderful friends." As the smell of beer and grease wafted in the air at the Hare and Stag pub, Chaney Sullivan raised a pint of ale in honor of the twelve co-workers sitting around the table for her going-away party. Her chest tightened at the thought of leaving London. "I'm going to miss you all so much."

"Just wait until we show up on your doorstep wanting to go to Disneyland." Gemma, who rented a room to Chaney, tossed her mane of blond hair behind her shoulder. "You won't be missing us then."

"Disneyland, Universal Studios, Beverly Hills, Venice Beach." The thought of seeing these people again brought a ball of warmth to the center of Chaney's chest. She set her glass on the table. "I'm happy to play tour guide if any of you come visit Los Angeles."

"Does that include me?" a deep male voice said from behind her.

The familiar Welsh accent filled her tummy with butterflies. The flapping of their wings matched the speed of her pulse.

She stood, turned and faced Drake Llewelyn, CEO of Dragon Llewelyn Limited. The top of her head came to his chin, and she stared up at him.

His glossy-magazine-model good looks and athletic build, hidden beneath an expensive tailored suit, always brought oohs and ahs from females. His way of making each employee feel as if they were the key to his company's success had earned him the gratitude of all who worked for him regardless of gender. But in Chaney's opinion his can-do attitude and work ethic were what made the man.

At twenty-nine years old—only seven years older than she was herself—he'd built Dragon Llewelyn into a successful multinational corporation with a global portfolio of media and telecommunications businesses. This he'd done through a combination of raw sweat and street smarts.

Her smile widened with admiration. She couldn't help herself.

He looked every inch a power broker, except for one thing—his hair. No neatly trimmed above the collar, corporate style for him. His dark wavy locks fell past his collar in the back, making him look more rakish than respectable.

She'd imagined running her fingers through his hair more than once. She'd imagined herself doing a lot of things with him. None of which had anything to do with her internship responsibilities.

He raised a brow, as if waiting for an answer. Which he was, she realized. Drake Llewelyn didn't like waiting for anything or anyone. In the four months she'd been interning in the mergers and acquisitions department, she'd learned that much about him.

Chaney lifted her chin, acting bolder than she felt. The beer, she wondered, or maybe the realization she would be an ocean and continent away from him tomorrow night. "Of course that includes you, Mr. Llewelyn."

"Drake," he corrected. "As of an hour ago, your internship ended. You no longer work for me."

His warm brown eyes with golden flecks gazed into hers, making Chaney feel as if she were the next special project he wanted to tackle. Her insides quivered.

Not that he would, with the bevy of beautiful women he dated and a supermodel currently being deemed his girlfriend *du jour* by the media.

But the thought raised Chaney's temperature ten degrees. If this were a birthday party instead of a going-away party, she knew what she'd wish for when blowing out the candles.

"Drake." She forced the name from her parched throat, feeling more like a tweener with her first crush than a twenty-two year old woman. Okay, she did have a huge crush on him, as did every other female who worked at the company. Probably every woman who breathed, no matter what age or marital status.

The man was a catch.

His chiseled cheekbones and jaw tempted a woman to reach out and touch them. His full lips hinted at long, hot kisses. And his bank account promised a life free from financial worry.

Prince Charming had nothing on Drake Llewelyn. He was King Midas and Adonis rolled into one. What woman wouldn't want to be the one who captured his heart?

"Make a note of our new travel guide in Southern California, Gem," he said in that half-teasing, half-serious tone Chaney had come to know and love. "With a cable channel in our portfolio now, we may be spending more time there."

Adoration filled Gemma's eyes. She, too, had fallen under the spell of the dragon, Drake's nickname in the office. She batted her lashes and flashed a smile. "Already noted, sir."

"Very good." His easy smile crinkled the corners of his eyes.

Chaney bit back a sigh. She'd been longing for the unattainable—okay, him—since she met him on the third day of her internship.

Gemma scooted a chair to the table, right between hers and Chaney's. Everyone else seemed more interested in filling their pints than staring at their gorgeous boss.

"But we're not here to watch football on the telly." Drake motioned to the table littered with half-filled glasses and plates of French fries. "A bon voyage party needs more than beer and chips. I'll be right back."

He strode away and spoke to the bartender. Soon plates of appetizers arrived along with bottles of champagne and glasses. The table resembled a buffet. Leave it to Mr. Llewelyn—make that Drake.

"Now we can send Chaney back to the States in style," he said with a satisfied smile.

A barmaid handed her a glass of champagne.

"This is so…" Chaney felt as light and carefree as the bubbles floating to the top of her glass, but she didn't want to sound starstruck even if she felt that way inside. "…thoughtful of you, sir. Thank you."

"It's the least I can do after the hard work and long hours you've put in these past months, especially with the acquisition of the cable channel." Drake raised his glass. "To Chaney, who will be missed."

Her co-workers raised their champagne flutes and repeated the cheer.

Tears stung Chaney's eyes. Her tongue felt two sizes too big. This was more of a sendoff than she could imagine. She muttered her gratitude and sipped her champagne.

He handed her a white handkerchief, the kind her grandfather had kept in his back pocket. She never thought a younger man like Drake would carry one, too. The chivalrous, old-fashioned gesture brought another well of tears.

Drake Llewelyn was almost too good to be true.

As Chaney dabbed her eyes with the cloth, her friends attacked the food like a pack of starving hyenas. She didn't blame them. Everything looked delicious and smelled good, too.

"Aren't you going to eat?" Drake asked.

She nodded. "I'm trying to figure out what I want to try first."

"I know what I want."

"The shrimp?"

He moved closer, so close his warm breath fanned her neck, and the male scent of him surrounded her. "Too much garlic."

Chaney shivered, a combination of excitement and fear. She was used to swooning from afar, not up close and personal. Though she worked on the same floor as him, their interactions had been limited to meetings and a few conversations in the hallway. Still she mustered her courage. "So what appeals to you, Drake?"

"You."

The air whooshed from her lungs. This couldn't be happening. She clenched her fists, digging her fingernails into her palms. Ouch. At least she wasn't dreaming. "I, um…"

"I've been watching you," he said quietly, regarding her over his champagne glass. "You're smart, hardworking and sexy as hell. Don't go back to the States, Chaney. Stay here in London with me."

Her heart beat in triple time. Who was she kidding? The hammering of her heart was probably taking years off her life, but she didn't care. Drake Llewelyn wanted her to stay in London. He must have broken up with the supermodel.

Anticipation danced through Chaney. Excitement, too. All the time she'd been dreaming about him, she had no idea he'd noticed her as anything other than one of the interns. "Why didn't you say anything?"

"You do work for me, darling. Did," he corrected himself. "I'm not in the habit of dating employees."

None of her daydreams had ever been this good. Nothing in her life had ever made her feel so good.

Chaney wiggled her toes. But she'd better not get too far ahead of herself.

"You really want me to stay?" she asked.

"Absolutely."

Oh, wow. She wanted to stay in London. With him. Mrs. Drake Llewelyn. She inhaled deeply and exhaled slowly. "For how long?"

His brow slanted. "For as long as we're both having fun."

Fun. She thought about his answer, repeated the words in her head. For as long as we're both having fun.

Drake didn't want forever; he wanted to have fun. What he really wanted, she realized, was sex. And then move on to the woman who caught his eye, the same way he had in the months she'd worked for him, the same way he did with the companies he bought, restructured and sold for a megaprofit once the newness wore off.

Disappointment ripped through Chaney. The legs of the pedestal she'd placed him on crumbled. She straightened.

No more getting carried away where Drake was concerned. She pressed her toes firmly to the bottom of her boots. No more crush, either. She wasn't any man's plaything.

What had she been thinking? The guy wasn't a catch. He might be gorgeous. He might be rich.

But he probably still had a girlfriend, too. That would make him a cheater.

Disgust slithered down her spine.

Drake Llewelyn was nothing but a player, a man who thought nothing of going through a slew of women all in the name of having "fun."

"Sorry, Mr. Llewellyn." Chaney squared her shoulders. "You're targeting the wrong girl. Short-term investments, however appealing, are too risky for me. I'm only interested in a long-term investment strategy."

CHAPTER ONE

"DAMSEL in distress here." Struggling to carry a heavy box full of what felt like bricks, Chaney eyed the row of antique armor on display in the great hall of Abbotsford Castle. "Hey, knights in shining armor. Can I get some help please?"

The polished suits stood at attention, weapons in hand as if ready for battle, but not one moved.

The story of her life. Chaney laughed.

Okay, she might not have the happily ever-after ending she once thought she'd have, but she couldn't complain too much. Not many people got to fly to London and stay at a luxurious castle with all expenses paid while working as the associate producer on a highly rated cable channel show for three days.

This was the kind of hands-on production experience her boss, Justin, said she needed if she wanted to have a shot at the promotion she'd been eyeing. Okay, dreaming about since the job notice appeared and she'd started filling in the application. Knowing finance was one thing, but knowing how projects got made and being in the trenches on a set was another. That was why he let her use her vacation days to come to England this week.

And she had one person to thank for the opportunity.

Gemma.

Her friend and former roommate was counting on Chaney to make sure the taping of *The Billionaire's Playground*, a travel show profiling the vacation spots of the uber-wealthy, went off without a hitch. Gemma's job required her to look out for the cable channel's interest, to put out fires and most importantly make sure the show stayed on budget and on schedule. Chaney wouldn't let her friend down.

The container full of electrical gear slipped in Chaney's sweaty hands. Her arm muscles strained against the weight. Her eyeglasses slid down her nose.

Dropping the hefty box on the gleaming wood floor would be an expensive no-no, one that could have historical implications given the medieval age of the castle. She tightened her grip, but it didn't help.

"May I help you, my lady?" a male voice asked from behind her.

The Welsh accent reminded her of Drake Llewelyn, but Gemma had said another billionaire would probably host this episode because he had a previous engagement. Chaney had been relieved to know she wouldn't have to see him again.

"Thank you." She rested the container against her bended knee. "I should have borrowed a baggage cart or dolly."

"Allow me."

She glanced back at her rescuer. A man wearing chain mail, black leather and armor plates on his shoulders, chest and legs approached. And not just any man...

Drake Llewelyn.

Her breath caught in her throat. He looked like a knight from King Arthur's Round Table, not a billionaire businessman whose latest pet project had him hosting a travel show for his cable channel.

She had to admit the look suited him. Awareness fluttered through her.

Too bad Drake Llewelyn wasn't a noble knight. He didn't follow any code of chivalry. His armor should be tarnished, not polished. She really shouldn't care what he looked like.

He walked toward her with the grace and agility of an athlete. The armor didn't slow him down one bit.

Uh-oh. She stiffened with apprehension. The

costume must mean he was hosting this episode after all. That meant she would be working with him for the next three days.

"Hello, Chaney."

The warm sound of his voice seeped through her. He took the box out of her arms as if it weighed no more than a container of laundry detergent.

She pushed her glasses back into the place. Her tired and dry eyes had made her take out her contact lenses three hours ago. "Thanks."

"Thank you for coming at such short notice and filling in for Gem," he said. "Are you up to speed on the show and this episode?"

Her heart thudded. "Yes."

Though the show was the last thing on her mind at the moment.

Two familiar brown eyes, with gold flecks flickering like flames, stared into hers and sent Chaney's temperature soaring. His mussed hair made him look as if he'd just returned to the castle after a crusade and was ready to bed the first female who caught his eye. And his beard…

She did a double take. He'd always been clean shaven before. "You grew a beard."

"For the taping." Drake ran his fingers over the hair on his chin. "Not as full as I'd hoped, but I thought a beard would look more knightly."

"It does." She normally didn't like men with

facial hair, but the mustache and beard, combined with the costume, made Drake look dark, dangerous and sexy. A black knight who, no doubt, had his pick of maidens, courtesans and queens.

Chaney swallowed around the crown-jewel-size lump in her throat.

"Where would you like the box?" he asked.

The deep rumble of his voice coupled with his accent made her stomach cartwheel and do a series of backflips like a gymnast during a floor exercise routine. The unexpected reaction put every one of her nerve endings on alert.

"By the lights." Her voice sounded low, almost husky and totally unnatural. The same odd way it felt to be giving Drake Llewelyn orders or feeling the bolt of unwelcome attraction. She cleared her dry throat. "Please place the box next to the lights."

As he carefully set the box where one of tonight's scenes would be taped, chain mail clinked. The sound echoed through the cavernous hall until swallowed up by the tapestry-covered walls.

Drake stood, looking taller than she remembered. She hadn't remembered his eyelashes being so thick and long, either. He seemed more handsome, if that were possible.

Maybe she was more tired than she realized. Exhaustion could easily explain her reaction to him.

His gaze raked over Chaney.

She crossed her arms over her chest. "If I'd known we were supposed to dress up, I would have brought my beer wench costume."

Drake laughed. "It's been too long, Chaney."

Five years, one month and, she did a quick calculation, about five days. Not long enough in her opinion. "I'm only here as a favor for Gemma."

"It's still good to see you again."

No way would she allow herself to be charmed by him. Being enticed by his knight get-up was bad enough. She straightened. "I doubt you missed me."

"But I have."

"Not according to the tabloids."

He adjusted one of the chain mail sleeves, as if the leather pants, tunic and armor were his daily attire not a designer suit from Brioni. "You've been following me in the tabloids?"

"Not really. Just…when I'm in line at the grocery store." And drawn to the stories of Drake dating women as if they were library books to be checked out and returned before their due date. A leopard didn't change its spots, and so it seemed, neither did a dragon.

"Grocery shopping. For your family?"

Her chest tightened. "Myself."

"Gemma told me you were engaged." He

glanced at her left hand, at her bare ring finger to be exact. "I thought you'd be married by now."

Her, too. "Nope."

"Let me guess, you found the long-term investment strategy lacking."

Her cheeks burned when she remembered what she'd said to him five years ago. If she'd known then... Who was she kidding? She probably wouldn't have done anything differently.

"No," Chaney admitted. "He did."

Drake reached his hand toward her, but she stepped away from him. "Chaney—"

"I'm not looking for sympathy," she interrupted. "I got enough of that when Tyler, my fiancé, broke up with me."

"I wasn't going to say I'm sorry, because I'm not. The man is obviously an idiot."

She bit back a smile. She'd forgotten how Drake could put things into perspective with only a few words. "He married my sister."

"Then your brother-in-law is an idiot," Drake said.

Chaney laughed. "You're right about that."

"You're too young to settle down."

"Well, I don't plan on settling down anytime soon."

"We have something in common."

"That makes two things," she said.

Drake gave her a puzzled look.

"Gemma." Chaney picked up her clipboard from the top of the box. "We have her in common."

His eyes darkened. "Yes, we do."

"I don't see her much, but thank goodness for the Internet. I don't know what I would do without her."

"Me, neither."

The emotion in the two words, as well as the concern in his eyes, caught her off guard. "You know, Gemma's going to be fine. Her baby, too. I spoke with her this morning after I arrived. She is sure the bed rest is temporary, and with the way Oliver is spoiling her, she'll be good to go for the rest of this season's tapings."

"Let's hope so, but until then…" A smile touched Drake's lips. "I have you."

The approval in his eyes let Chaney know he liked what he saw. She wouldn't let herself care.

"Only on the set," she said crisply.

"Of course." His eyes laughed at her.

Flustered, she clutched her clipboard. "I'll make sure things stay on schedule so you can catch your flight out of Heathrow. Gemma said that was important."

"Still the same industrious, competent Chaney. This arrangement should work out well."

She raised her chin. "I think so."

His lips curved into a full smile, showing two rows of straight, white teeth. He did have a nice smile. "I always knew you'd go far, but I thought you were going to work with your father, not take your financial skills and go into show business."

"Well, my parents did name me after Lon Chaney," she admitted.

"Lon Chaney, that old actor?"

"They were die-hard horror fans, but preferred the older black-and-white flicks to the newer slasher movies." She remembered how Drake had kept their conversations focused on business when she was an intern. Well, except for her going-away party. "I once called my mom 'mummy' and she gave me a cookie."

"That's—"

"Weird, I know, but Chaney's better than Karloff or Lorre. Though Bela might not have been too bad," she admitted. "But in spite of my name, I actually got my first taste of television during my internship when you acquired the Dragon Network. That experience led me to the job at the studio where I work."

"It's amazing how an internship can change a career path."

He had no idea. She nodded.

"And now you're back in England working on the show we brainstormed."

Her mouth gaped. She closed it. "You remember?"

"Your name is in the credits."

"That was a nice gesture, but it's not the same show we'd talked about."

"Maybe not, but *The Billionaire's Playground* wouldn't exist if not for that meeting you attended."

His words meant a lot to her and echoed what Gemma had said. "Thank you."

"So how does it feel?" Drake asked.

"Pretty cool." Chaney wiggled her toes. "I remember watching the premiere episode and thinking, wow, this is what all those ideas we were tossing back and forth turned into. Though I never thought you'd host the show."

"Me, neither," he admitted. "But I had a free weekend when they were set to shoot the pilot. We hadn't found the right talent to host, and Gem said I should do it. I had fun, so I decided to make it a regular gig. Though we've started using guest hosts."

"Gemma told me."

"Do you have a favorite episode?" he asked.

"I'd have to say it's the one with kite surfing on the coast of Greenland."

"That was an exciting episode to tape," he said. "The Google guys took a vacation there and gave us the idea."

"Whose idea was it to use a medieval castle this weekend?"

"Gem after she nixed my idea of base-jumping in Norway."

"Good call," Chaney said. "Previews of you in your knight costume will bring in viewers and increase ratings a lot more than you doing a crazy stunt."

He raised a brow. "You sound confident."

"It's my job to understand viewers and translate ratings into advertising revenue," she explained. "All you have to do is take a look at yourself in any one of the gilded mirrors around here. The knight look will be huge with female viewers. You may span a whole new following with Sir Dragon Knight."

He laughed. "And I thought women were only after my bank account."

"I'm sure there are those, too, but all women are susceptible to the archetype of a knight. Even if they'd never admit it."

"Do you admit it?" he asked.

"Well, I definitely had a thing for knights when I was younger. Galahad was my favorite, but the whole fairy-tale thing seems a bit…outdated. I don't need anyone to rescue me. I can do it myself."

Even if she still might dream of a happily ever after of her own someday.

"Very modern. Very practical."

"I am practical." She'd had to be. "Anything wrong with that?"

"Nothing at all." The devilish look in his brown eyes matched the grin on his face. "I'm curious how your practicality has affected your current investment strategy philosophy. Do you prefer short term, long term or day trading?"

"None of the above." She raised her chin and met his inquisitive gaze. "I'm currently on hiatus from…investing."

Talk about a marathon session tonight. Drake had almost been grateful when the clock struck midnight and the chimes interrupted the taping.

Of course he was the executive producer as well as the host, or talent as the crew called it. He could have shut down production at any time except he had a helicopter to catch on Sunday afternoon so he could make a flight at Heathrow. He didn't want to cause any delays.

Hot lights shone on him. Sweat dripped down his armor-clad body. Even though he was wearing a costume, the armor was metal not plastic. Drake was going to need a shower, and maybe a massage, when they were finished. He knew exactly who he wanted to help him with both.

Drake couldn't see Chaney Sullivan. He surveyed the drawing room looking for a peek of her caramel-colored hair, but couldn't see her with the two cameras in front of him and the crew milling about behind them. Maybe she was hidden in the back.

The antique one-of-a-kind clock continued to chime. Ten, eleven, twelve...

Quiet. Finally.

"Okay, people." Milt, the director and producer, clapped his hands. "Let's get this final scene wrapped up so we can call it a night."

Drake was all for that.

"One sec." The hair-and-makeup stylist, a woman named Liz who preferred soda to wine and pretzels to caviar, ran up to him. She fluffed, finger curled and sprayed his hair, making him feel like a fancy show dog. She smiled, satisfaction filling her eyes. "That's better."

For her maybe. At least the wardrobe stylist, a guy named Russell, wasn't trying to spit shine the armor. Just buff it with a soft, white cloth.

"We only need the last line," Milt said.

Drake stretched his neck. "No problem."

"That's what I like to hear." Milt's eyes narrowed. "I only want you to do one thing differently this time. When you smile at the camera, make it really count. Make the female viewers wet between the legs."

"I'm a businessman, not an actor."

"You're neither of those things tonight." As Milt patted Drake's shoulder, his ring clanged against the armor. "You're Lancelot, knight and lover extraordinaire. Guinevere, your queen, is alone in the castle, naked in her bed, and watching you. Make her wish you were there with her."

Drake fought the urge to roll his eyes. And laugh.

This part of show business was something he would never understand. Still, doing the show was good publicity and PR for the channel and his company. He trusted his gut, and his instinct said do what Milt wanted. That was what Drake had done for the past two seasons and saw no need to change now. "You're in charge, but let's hope Guin's covered herself with a blanket. Castles can be drafty this time of year."

The crew laughed. Even Milt cracked a smile.

Liz came after Drake with the eyelash curler. "I forgot something."

"Is that really necessary again?" he asked.

She winked. "Absolutely, Sir Lashalot."

Drake grimaced, allowed the deed to be done and readied himself for the scene.

Holding a gold goblet precariously with his gauntlet-covered hand, he stood in front of an elaborately carved fireplace complete with an ornate coat of arms being held by two lion-faced cherubim.

"Ready, Sir Lancelot?" Milt asked.

Drake nodded once.

Milt looked at Tony, one of the two cameramen on the crew. "Let me know when you have speed."

"Are the mikes working?" Tony asked the audio person, who gave him the thumbs-up. "Speed."

A few seconds later, Drake saw his cue.

Show time.

Once he nailed this line, he'd be free to do whatever he wanted. And he knew what—make that who—he wanted.

Forget Guinevere.

The adulterous queen had nothing on his new associate producer. An image of Chaney wearing her sexy, smart-girl glasses flashed in his mind.

He raised the goblet and smiled at the camera. "And that's why Abbotsford Castle is one of this billionaire's favorite playgrounds."

Luxurious and romantic, this castle would be the perfect place to play with Chaney. Five years hadn't changed the smart, pretty American's appeal.

Drake still wanted to taste those full, pink lips of hers that had tempted him during her internship. He wanted to see if the adorable dimple on her left cheek went as deep as it looked. He wanted to lend a hand as she wiggled out of those well-fitted jeans, cupping her bottom like a glove, so he could see if she wore a thong, boy short or other type of panty underneath.

Most of all, he hadn't forgotten the way she'd turned him down.

Sorry Mr. Llewelyn. You're targeting the wrong girl.

He'd been sorry all right especially since he'd stopped dating a woman, a supermodel if he remembered correctly, to pursue Chaney. But she hadn't wanted him.

Drake had thought about that, about her, over the years. Now that he'd seen her again, and found out she wasn't married as he'd believed, he wanted another chance.

Before the weekend was over, Drake wanted to hear the word "yes" fall from Chaney's lips. A "please take me now" wouldn't be so bad, either. He wanted to prove to himself and her that he hadn't targeted the wrong girl. Far from it. Given the antics and partying that accompanied the production crew during their two and a half months on the road, he had high hopes.

His smile widened.

Milt counted down with his fingers. Five-four-three-two-one.

"Cut! That's a wrap people." Milt adjusted his LA Dodgers baseball cap. "Perfect, Drake. Keep smiling like that, and you'll be a lock making this year's Sexiest Man Alive list."

Drake handed the goblet to Jesse, an intern

working on the show, and took a bottle of water from her. "Thanks, but I'd rather top the Richest Man Alive list."

As he downed the water, the crew, including a few locals hired to help due to the size of the castle and amount of work involved in this particular episode, moved gear in preparation for tomorrow's shoot. The show had exclusive use of the castle for the next two days so they didn't have to worry about anyone getting in the way. The castle staff had experience with film crews so would be no trouble.

He handed his empty bottle to Jesse, who scurried away to who knew where. Funny, but Drake couldn't remember the last time he'd had to find a garbage can himself. Years ago, he'd dug through trash cans out of necessity for him and his dad. How times had changed.

As he made his way past the lights and cameras, he searched for Chaney. He found her standing in the doorway with her clipboard in hand and talking to the production coordinator. As he crossed the drawing room in her direction, desire rocketed through him.

He'd appreciated Chaney's athletic all-American girl figure before, but now her clothes accentuated fuller curves. Her long hair worn in braids or a ponytail had always looked charming on the college co-ed, but the new sophisticated shoulder-length cut suited her face better. The biggest and most intriguing change, though, was to her eyes. Not the glasses, but the maturity he saw in the hazel-green depths.

Chaney Sullivan was no longer a girl. She'd become a woman. A woman who was hardworking, confident and, most important, smart. Her intelligence had always been the draw for him, Drake realized, even if he liked the package it came in, too.

He slowed his approach until the production coordinator walked away. By then most of the crew had left. "Hello, there."

"Hi." Chaney held her clipboard in front of her like a barrier between them. A barrier he had every intention of breaking down. "Great job tonight."

"Thank you."

She stifled a yawn.

Chaney should be in bed. His bed, if Drake had his choice. "Join me for a drink?"

"I thought you didn't date employees."

"I don't."

"Uh-huh."

She was considered an independent contractor, and her paycheck would be coming from the cable channel as Gemma's did, not the corporate office. So Chaney was, in effect, fair game. "You don't work for me."

"Not officially, but I'm—"

"Tired?"

"Exhausted."

"I'll have to let you go, then. But could you do a little something for me first, please?"

She readied her pen over her clipboard. "Sure, what do you need?"

Staring into her eyes, he smiled. "I need your help getting out of this costume."

CHAPTER TWO

UNDRESS him? Chaney's heart pounded in her ears. Surely she had misunderstood. "You want me to…"

"Help me out of this armor," Drake finished for her. "I don't know where Russell ran off to, and you're the only one left."

She glanced around the drawing room, now deserted. Where had everyone gone? The room had been bustling with activity a few minutes ago.

He stared at her, an expectant look in his brown eyes.

Face it, Gemma wouldn't think twice about helping him. Neither should Chaney. He'd made a reasonable request, and she was acting as if he'd asked her to his room for a night of hot sex. Sure, the man oozed sensuality, but just because he'd wanted her once didn't mean he wanted her now.

Time to stop overreacting and do her job.

Chaney straightened. "What do you want me to do first?"

"Come with me."

She fell in step with Drake, noticing he shortened his stride to match hers. He'd always had lovely, rather Old World manners. She remembered the handkerchief he'd once offered her. Of course, that had been right before he propositioned her.

"Where are we going?" she asked.

"To my room."

Her heart bumped. Okay, he was inviting her to his room, but sex was not on the agenda. Hers or, she hoped, his.

No worries, Chaney told herself. She'd heard he was staying in the king's bedchamber and knew only a staircase led to the suite, not an elevator. He probably didn't feel like stripping out of the armor and carrying it up to his room. She wouldn't, either.

No big deal going up there with Drake. She would help him out of the costume then head to her room for some much-needed and well-earned sleep.

She yawned. The jet lag had finally caught up with her. "Will this take long?"

"It shouldn't," he said.

Relieved, Chaney stepped through an arched doorway into a hallway of stone. Stone walls, floor and ceiling surrounded her. Electric torches illuminated a circular staircase in front of her. She shivered. Those stone steps led to one place—Drake's room.

Stop being melodramatic. No big deal, remember. It wasn't as if she were going to be locked away in a tower cell with him. She was just going up there to help him undress. Chaney gulped.

Drake gestured up the narrow staircase. "After you."

"Thanks, but I don't know the way," she demurred. "My flight was delayed so I missed the taping of the guest rooms this morning. Is it true Henry VIII slept in the king's bedchamber?"

"That's what they say." As Drake ascended, his armor and chain mail clanked. The sound echoed through the stairwell. "He seems to have slept his way across England."

She followed Drake up. "He did have six wives."

"Six too many."

"Divorced, beheaded, died, divorced, beheaded, survived." Chaney repeated the rhyme she'd memorized back in school. "I'm sure at least half of them would agree with you."

"All of them should."

The disdain in his voice surprised her. She remembered what he'd said earlier today in the great hall. "So you're not interested in settling down or in marriage?"

"Beheadings, divorces and deaths sound about right when it comes to matrimony."

"Don't forget one of Henry's wife survived those fates."

"Sheer luck." He glanced back at Chaney. "I prefer better odds."

His take on marriage brought a twinge of disappointment, but she didn't know why. "Don't you want a family?"

He shrugged. "I have no time for a family."

"Someday then?"

He continued up the stairs, all armor and wide shoulders. "Perhaps, but I don't see it happening."

"You never know what might happen." The torches flickered like candles, casting shadows through the stairwell. She touched the wall, the stone cool and rough beneath her palm. "It almost feels as if we've gone back in time."

"Except this castle has electricity, heating, indoor plumbing and Wi-Fi."

"My kind of castle."

"Mine, too," he admitted. "Though there is something to be said for a time when men were men. That isn't always the case today."

Armor aside, Drake was as manly as men came. "Many of those men didn't live to see middle age, let alone old age."

"True, but at least there were rules and codes to

battles as well as relationships. That had to make things easier."

"Easier doesn't sound very romantic."

"Let me guess." His lighthearted tone teased. "You're one of those romantic women who enjoy hearts, flowers and violins."

"Well, I'm not all that into hearts and violins, but I do like flowers. If that makes me one of those romantic women, so be it." She climbed the stairs behind him. "I do believe true love exists."

"Love may exist," he admitted. "But I don't think it lasts long in the real world or really offers much."

"My parents are still together after thirty-two years of marriage," Chaney countered. "I doubt they made it that far by simply liking each other."

"Like can go a long way. As can habit." Drake reached the top of the stairs. "But I hope for your parents' sake and for Gemma and Oliver's, that their love lasts."

Maybe Drake wasn't all that bad. He obviously cared about Gemma's happiness and future, but his words still bothered Chaney. "So you're not a full-blown cynic about love."

He stood in front of a massive wood door, looking every inch the lord of the manor or, in this case, king of the castle. "I prefer to think of myself as a realist."

"We should agree to disagree, then, because I feel totally removed from reality right now."

Smiling, he pushed down on the door handle. "Then enjoy the fantasy."

The words *Drake* and *fantasy* did not belong in the same sentence. Okay, the guy might be a total hottie and physically appealing, but Chaney disagreed with everything he said about the subjects of love and marriage. Even though she didn't want to settle down now, that didn't mean not ever. One day she hoped to experience the kind of love that lasted, the forever kind. And she would never want to date a man who had such different views on relationships from her. Not that Drake wanted to date her.

He opened the door.

"You don't lock your room?" she asked.

"Can't. No place to put the key."

"You could have asked one of us to hold it."

"The castle is secure. The production crew top rate. Even the locals we've hired seem like excellent workers." He held the door for her. "Besides I don't have anything that can't be replaced."

Chaney tried to understand his way of thinking. Tried and failed. "One of the perks of being wealthy, I'd imagine."

"For me, yes." He didn't sound boastful, simply honest. "Others might disagree."

"Several others, I'd imagine."

"Yourself."

It wasn't a question. "I don't have expensive

jewelry or electronics with me, but what I have I'd like to keep."

"If I were yours, I'd want to be kept."

Her cheeks warmed. Chaney crossed the threshold to his room so he wouldn't see her blush. She couldn't imagine Drake allowing any woman to keep him. Especially her. "Wow. Now I know what the production coordinator meant when she called this room opulent."

No expense had been spared in decorating the suite, a series of rooms, each of which was larger than Chaney's one-bedroom apartment in Los Angeles. She stood in the sitting area, where a fire burned in the hand-carved fireplace. The golden flames added warmth and a romantic atmosphere.

Not romantic, she corrected. Nothing about her being her could be construed as romantic. She was here to do a job, nothing else.

Still she caught a glimpse of the bedroom off to her right. Gold and Wedgwood-blue silk curtains hung from a large canopy bed, a bed fit for royalty, heads of state or a corporate raider. Coordinating pillows made a pair of overstuffed chairs placed beneath an arched window look even more luxurious.

"This suite is so lavish," Chaney said.

"It is rather regal looking." He removed his

gauntlets and placed them on a round table. "If you like it so much, we can trade rooms."

"Thanks, but I'm happy where I am." Coming back to England had been a good move, even with seeing Drake again. She'd been handed a golden excuse to miss the housewarming party at her sister's new house this weekend. No having to tell friends and family she still didn't have a boyfriend and that she wasn't jealous her sister was living in a beautiful house in Malibu with a view and a guesthouse. Nope, this was much better than that anyday. "You belong here. This is the king's bedchamber."

Drake bowed. "I am but a mere knight, my lady."

"A king in knight's clothing." And with a kingly bed. Chaney noticed the bedding had been turned down. The sheets must be at least 400-count Egyptian cotton. "You shouldn't sleep anywhere but here."

"It is a comfortable room."

"Comfortable? It's so spectacular I'm afraid to touch anything. I bet that table-and-chair set is worth more than I am." She pointed the clipboard toward a four-foot-high vase on her left. "That vase probably costs more than my annual salary."

"Don't worry," he said. "We were required to take out a large insurance rider in order to use the castle and grounds for the show. You're safe."

She didn't feel so safe. Her gaze strayed to his inviting bed. Her bed would look just as good, she reminded herself.

"It's late." Chaney's heavy eyelids kept wanting to close. The sooner she got to her own room, the better. She set her clipboard on the table. "Let me help you out of your costume so we can get to bed."

"My bed or yours?"

Heat flamed her cheeks. "You know what I meant."

"I always like to make sure and remove any doubt. It saves me from misunderstandings down the road as well as missed opportunities."

"You're not missing anything with me." The words tumbled from her mouth. "I mean…"

Amusement gleamed in his eyes. "What do you mean, Chaney?"

He sounded so cool and collected, as if having a member of the opposite sex in his room after midnight was no big deal.

Okay, it probably wasn't to him.

Still, the way he stood there looking sexier than anyone had a right to look dressed like a character from a summer blockbuster movie irritated Chaney.

No, he irritated her.

And that's when she realized…

She was still angry with him for what happened five years ago, for shattering her illusion of him.

She'd wanted to find her Prince Charming back then. She'd wanted him to be Drake. Instead she'd returned home and met Tyler, a man totally opposite from Drake. A man she'd thought had loved her. At least, he'd claimed to love her until he met Simone.

Chaney tucked her hair behind her ears. "How do you remove the costume?"

Drake lifted his left arm and pointed with his right hand. "Buckles are hidden underneath. They attach the armor pieces. You have to undo them."

Okay, that didn't sound difficult.

As she walked toward him, heat hit her. Not from the fireplace, but from Drake. She knew he was hot, but not literally. Heat emanated from him. His scent, sweaty, musky and male, filled her nostrils.

"I'm looking forward to getting out of this costume and into a shower," he said.

She did not want to think about him naked with warm water shooting down on him. She glanced at the bed again. Thinking about him there probably wasn't a good idea, either.

Chaney pulled apart the armor plates to find the buckles. "All I want to do is sleep."

"That bed does look…inviting. They even left chocolate on the pillows." He stared down at her. "Two chocolates."

Uh-oh. She undid a buckle. "The staff may have assumed you'd have company."

"I do. Are you interested?"

Her fingers fumbled. "What?"

His eyes danced with laughter. "In a chocolate."

"I'm not company. I work for your company." Unfastening another buckle, her fingertips brushed the chain mail underneath. "How many layers are you wearing?"

"A few, but once the chain mail is off, I can handle the rest. Unless you'd rather help with that, too."

Her fingers trembled. No way would she respond to him. Anything she said would come out wrong and might even sound as if she were interested in helping with…more. She pressed her lips together.

Chaney focused on the armor, not the man underneath it. She caught glimpses of chain mail, a quilted shirt, dark hair. Intriguing images. Tempting impressions. Ones she ignored. She unbuckled the pieces around his chest and shoulders and placed each in a special container sitting on the floor of his room.

She knelt at his feet to remove the lower half of the armor. Reaching around his thigh, she found her hands between his legs and her head much too close to his, um, codpiece.

"I appreciate this, Chaney," he said as if she

were tying his shoes, not practically fondling him as she tried to reach a buckle. "I know you're tired."

She kept her eyes focused on the buckle, not allowing herself to look anywhere else. Or touch any part of him. "Almost done."

Please, oh, please let me be almost done.

She hurriedly undid the buckle. Unfortunately, three more needed her attention and kept her in the uncomfortable, embarrassing position.

"All done," she said finally, laying the last piece of leg armor into its spot in the container.

"Thank you."

Chaney turned. The words "you're welcome" died on her parted lips.

Drake stood wearing chain mail that molded his muscular shoulders, arms and chest. The metal shirt fell to his hips. Talk about hot.

She swallowed.

He was every woman's fantasy and her worst nightmare. But that didn't stop her knees from going weak and her blood from boiling.

"The chain mail attaches in the back," he said.

Chaney forced herself into action. She fumbled with the first hook. Her fingers wouldn't do what she wanted them to do.

She blew out a frustrated breath.

Darn the man.

His soft-looking hair tempted her to touch it, to see if the strands would curl around her finger.

"Having trouble?" Drake asked.

He had no idea. "I'm getting there."

Or would. As soon as she reminded her traitorous body and out-of-control hormones she wasn't interested in Drake Llewelyn. He couldn't give her what she wanted: a forever kind of love. Not to mention she was taking a break from dating, from men.

An almost two-year break, a voice—maybe her heart—mocked.

Shut up.

"Excuse me?" he asked.

Oh, no. She hadn't meant to say that out loud. "Sorry, I was just trying to quiet the voices in my head."

"What were they saying?"

"That it was past my bedtime, but don't worry. I won't leave until the job is finished."

"I knew I could count on you."

Chaney didn't understand his confidence in her when she wasn't sure she could count on herself in this situation.

Finally the snap came undone. Slowly, much too slowly for her liking, she opened each of the remaining ones. "They're all unsnapped."

"Can you help me out of it?" Drake asked.

"Sure." Her voice sounded stronger than she felt. "Open the back."

As she did as he asked, Chaney realized how much the chain mail weighed. He shrugged out of the shirt so it rested on his upper arms.

"Now come around in front of me," he said. "Be careful, it's heavy."

Chaney held on to the shirt as he pulled one arm out and then another, never once leaving her to hold the entire weight of the chain mail.

He placed it in the container. His damp, quilted shirt clung to him. He pulled the tails out from the waistband of his pants. "Much better and cooler."

Maybe for him.

"I should go."

"Stay." One soft word in that sexy, accented voice.

She sucked in a breath. "But we're done."

His eyes lit again with that wicked, wicked laughter. "Darling, we're just getting started."

He walked—no, strutted—toward her, the set of his jaw full of purpose.

Drawn to his strength and heat, Chaney leaned toward him. She tilted her chin.

His gaze smoldered. His lips parted.

Chaney stood transfixed.

Drake stopped in front of her.

She could barely breathe, let alone think. She

stared up at him, confused, afraid, attracted. He lowered his mouth to hers.

He was going to kiss her.

The realization ricocheted through her brain. She wanted him to kiss her. Badly. Except...

She ducked her head and stepped back so the only thing his lips touched was air.

"I should *so* not be surprised by this." Her voice sounded shrill. She didn't care.

His head drew back. "Excuse me?"

"I probably shouldn't ask, given your reputation, but why would you choose to make a move on me now, when you know I'm so tired?"

"I thought you *wanted* me to kiss you."

She placed her hands on her hips. "Why would you think that?"

"The way you leaned toward me. The tilt of your head. The look in your eyes that said kiss me."

Oh, boy. Shame flooded her. She'd done all those things and probably more. "I'm sorry if I misled you."

"Don't be sorry." His smile could have charmed a starving mouse out of its last nibble of cheddar. "We can try again. Let me show you what you missed out on five years ago."

Sex. That was all he'd ever wanted from her.

Anger surged. Disappointment, too. She glanced to the bed and back at him. "In case you haven't figured it out, I'm not about to be another notch on your bedpost or wherever else you keep track of your conquests."

"If that's all I felt about you, Chaney, I wouldn't be here."

Even though she was upset at him, his words piqued her curiosity. "What are you talking about?"

"I decided to host this episode so I could see you again."

The air in his room sizzled. Drake saw a mix of disbelief and hope in Chaney's eyes. He wanted hope to win. That way he would win, too.

"You thought I was married and you still wanted to see me?" she asked.

"See you, yes. Nothing else."

"And if I hadn't agreed to fill in for Gemma?"

"But you did and you're here. Not to mention unmarried." He moved closer to her. "We've been given a second chance, Chaney. Let's make the most of this opportunity."

She put her hands on his chest to stop him. "Why don't you park yourself at the round table and cool down."

Her anger confused him. He hadn't expected that reaction.

She walked away from him. "You can't actually expect me to believe you."

"What I said is true."

Chaney gave him a look. "I only agreed to fill in for Gemma a few days ago. I realize you have enough money to have a custom suit of armor built for you at the last minute, but unless you've found a miracle formula to grow that much facial hair overnight, I'd say you spent well over a week on your beard. Probably longer than that."

Damn. Most women would have pretended not to see through what he'd said and play along, but not Chaney. Drake didn't know whether to be annoyed or amused by the turn of events. "You may have misunderstood my intentions."

"Oh, no. Your intentions are quite clear, but I want to make sure you don't misinterpret mine."

Forget annoyed. The way she dismissed him so easily and the strength she exhibited were total turn-ons.

She continued. "I'm sure whatever lines you normally use on women must work pretty well or you wouldn't be so confident, but just so you know, nothing's happening here tonight, tomorrow or any other day we happen to be in the same place."

No one ever challenged him like this. Maybe he should try another tack or perhaps cut his losses and send her on her way. The truth was he really didn't want her to leave. "Would you believe your being here gave me a reason to look forward to this weekend?"

Her clear, sharp eyes told him she wasn't about to be swayed by empty words or careless compliments.

Guilt lodged in his throat. "I'm sorry to have dragged you up here."

The tightness around her mouth told him he should be sorry. She picked up her clipboard from the table and headed toward the door.

"I'll walk you to your room," he offered.

"And tuck me in?" She pursed her lips. "No, thanks."

"I don't want you getting lost."

"I'll do fine on my own."

"You said you hadn't been to this part of the castle before."

"I can find my way down a lit stairwell."

The set of her jaw told him she wasn't about to back down. Early in life, he'd learned what battles were worth fighting. He knew this one wasn't. "Okay, you win."

For now.

Her tired eyes widened behind her glasses. "I didn't know it was a competition."

"Life is a competition."

"Only if you turn it into one."

Chaney may be tired, but her mind was fully

functioning. Still, he'd taken up enough of her time for tonight. Drake opened the door for her. "Thanks for your help. Get some sleep."

Not looking back at him, she fled down the staircase into the shadows.

Once she was out of sight, Drake closed the door.

Frustration gnawed at him. He hadn't been this off his game since Chaney's going-away party in London. But that experience hadn't left him feeling so damn guilty.

Regret swept over him. He'd taken advantage of her helpful nature to get her to his room. Not that she'd allowed him to take advantage of the situation at all.

He hadn't liked how she turned him down the last time, given her near hero worship of him five years ago, but he'd understood she wanted more than he was offering.

Tonight, however, stung. He rubbed his chin, still not used to the hair against his fingers. She'd been angry and dismissive. Something had changed. She had changed.

I'm on hiatus from…investing.

He knew who to blame….

Her stupid jerk of an ex-fiancé-turned-brother-in-law.

The guy must have hurt her bad. Her sister, too.

Drake grimaced.

Chaney might be a romantic, but she was a wounded one who needed to learn how to have fun again. That was why she reacted the way she had to his overtures.

All he had to do was figure out how to show her she needed some fun. She needed him.

Not an impossible task.

He'd done it before, with companies he'd purchased, by showing them he had something they needed. He would do the same thing with Chaney. A win-win situation for both of them.

And he knew exactly where to start. Drake picked up the telephone and pressed the button for the staff line.

"Good evening, Mr. Llewelyn," a proper-sounding male voice said. "What may I do for you?"

"Please deliver a large bouquet of flowers to Miss Sullivan's room tomorrow. In the morning, if possible."

"Roses?"

"No," Drake answered quickly. She would take roses the wrong way and rightfully so. "A mixed bouquet will be fine."

"What would you like written on the card, sir?"

He thought for a moment. "'Friends' with a question mark."

The man repeated the phrase.

"That's correct."

"I'll take care of this straight away, sir."

"Thank you." Drake hung up the phone.

Friends would be the perfect place to start with Chaney. Friends could have lots of fun together.

Staring at the armor she'd neatly put away for him, he smiled.

And if things worked out the way he planned, he and Chaney would be more than friends very, very soon.

CHAPTER THREE

CHANEY stood on the manicured lawn of the castle, her boots sinking into the sodden grass. A touch of foreboding in the air made it easy to forget the crew running around as they prepared for this morning's first scene.

She stared at the castle wall, rising up to meet the overcast sky. The ancient stones, battered by weather and war, had remained impenetrable, inviolate, over the centuries.

Shivering, she clutched her cup of Earl Gray. She'd forgotten how chilly English mornings could be.

Chaney had never been strong like the castle's wall. She'd always crumbled in the past, allowing people to break through her weak defenses and take what had been hers—a fiancé, a promised job, the dream of a happily ever after. Afterward, she would never say a word. Always the quiet one, forever the peacekeeper, bendable to a ridiculous degree, a proverbial doormat. That was what how she made those in her life, those who loved her, happy.

But the truth was she wanted to be more like the wall, solid and sure. That would make *her* happy.

The only person she'd ever been able to stand up to was Drake Llewelyn. And only twice. Five years ago and again last night.

His hitting on her as if she were still his naive intern infuriated Chaney. She had been even madder at herself for putting herself in a position where that could happen. Her anger had hardened her. Protected her from his charm.

Thank goodness.

Standing up to him, she'd felt strong, and she'd like that. Chaney resolved to be unbending, unconquerable and, for the remainder of the taping, immune to Drake.

The scent of green from the carpet of grass and rows of neatly clipped hedges filled the air.

She thought about the bouquet of flowers delivered to her room this morning with the one-word note—"Friends?" She couldn't imagine they were from Drake. The only kind of friend he would want was a friend with benefits. Gemma hadn't sent them. She would have sent something edible, most likely chocolate, as she always did. Not her parents, either. They hadn't been happy with Chaney when she canceled out on the house-warming party. Besides, they'd never sent her flowers before. Why start now?

Chaney had asked the castle desk about the flowers, and they promised the delivery had not been a mistake. But who would have sent them? And why?

A breeze rustled through a nearby tree. She looked up and saw the branches sway. Three leaves floated to the ground as the sky darkened on the horizon.

She eyed the heavy skies with misgiving, her hands still curled around her cup for warmth. She really hoped it didn't rain. A delay in the shooting schedule would force her to spend even more time with Drake. All she wanted was to do her job and avoid him as much as possible for the remainder of the shoot.

Milt motioned he was ready for the first take. The crew took their places and quieted.

She wasn't sure where this morning's scene would fit in the episode, a host shot or a wrap-around. Maybe a teaser of some sort.

One of the cameras panned across the land-scape, from the formal gardens to the acres of grass to a grove of trees. Something moved in the distance between the trees.

A white horse decked in armor.

And Drake, in his armor costume, on its back.

Despite the things he'd said and the way he'd acted last night, Chaney's breath caught in her throat. She'd thought he'd looked knightly yesterday, but today…

He was Lancelot. Okay, not Lancelot. But he sure did look the part.

Her heart thudded in her chest.

A helmet covered the sides of his jaw, but still showed most of his face. Not that she could see any details from this distance. Still she had no trouble imagining his lips with a wry curve to them and his dark eyes full of excitement.

He sat tall in the saddle, holding the reins in his left hand and a battle standard in his right. A long pennant-shaped banner flapped behind him.

The horse cantered through the trees to the lawn, animal and rider in perfect rhythm.

She stood mesmerized.

The air crackled, the impending storm or some sort of magic. Chaney didn't know which. But once again she felt as if she'd stepped back in time.

His gauntleted hand tightened on the reins as he sat back hard in the saddle. The horse tossed its head. Its armor jingled.

The knight raised the battle standard, a black dragon on a field of gold, before plunging the pole into the ground. The flag fluttered in the breeze. The horse arched its neck, dancing in place. The whole scene was like something from a movie or fairy tale, as far removed from Chaney's real life as it was possible to be.

And yet this man had tried to kiss her, had invited her to stay in his room last night.

Hot blood flooded her face and flowed through her veins.

"'My good blade carves the casques of men.'" His deep voice resonated, his words pure poetry. Tennyson's poem about Sir Galahad, in fact. Chaney recognized the poem from the script. The horse looked to the left and then pranced to the right. "'My tough lance thrusteth sure, My strength is as the strength of ten, Because my heart is pure.'"

Pure. Right.

This wasn't the Dragon Knight, a man who lived hundreds of years ago. This was Drake Llewelyn, a man from the twenty-first century.

He raised a shiny sword to the camera. His lips curved into the same come-hither-I-want-you-now smile he'd used in the drawing room and with her later in his room. The man was normally sexy, but practically smoldered now.

A good thing the noble-knight stuff was just an act, but even so, tingles filled her stomach.

As if on cue, a flock of birds flew overhead,

their dark wings a stark contrast against the gray clouds. The horse stamped its front hooves, ready to rear or run away if given the chance.

But Drake was in complete control.

As usual.

Whether on horseback or sitting at a table negotiating his next deal, he was comfortable in any environment. Sure of himself and strong. That was how *she* wanted to be.

Milt gave a signal.

Drake allowed the horse to rear. The horse looked majestic, nearly standing perpendicular on its hind legs.

Chaney's heart pounded in her ears. She knew Drake didn't mind taking risks, but she couldn't imagine him doing anything to endanger himself or the horse. Still every muscle tensed. She held her breath.

He didn't fall. Drake seemed to barely shift in his saddle.

Amazing. She didn't want to be impressed by anything he did, but she was. Anyone would be.

The horse lowered its front legs to the grass.

"Cut."

A smattering of applause from the crew filled the air. Chaney felt the urge to clap, too, but tightened her hands around her tea instead. She didn't want Drake to know she'd been watching him that closely. That she admired him at all. That she could reconsider his offer from last night. Because she was and she did and she wouldn't.

She couldn't.

Chaney wasn't the fling type.

Even if Drake wanted a relationship, which he didn't, a man like him could crush her heart. That was something she wanted to avoid happening at all costs. And she would do whatever it took to make sure that didn't happen.

She stared into her almost-empty cup.

"I never understood the appeal of a knight in shining armor before." Liz buttoned her long wool coat and raised the faux-fur collar. "But I do believe I have a new crush."

"Mine isn't so new," an intern named Jesse admitted in a crisp English accent. She'd taken fall semester off from college to work on the show.

"I'm not sure if it's the armor or the beard." Liz pursed her sparkling-with-gloss lips. "But I'm ready to ride off into the sunset with him."

Jesse muttered her agreement, never taking her eyes off Drake. She combed her gloved fingers through her long, blond hair.

As Chaney listened to the women, she remembered talking to Gemma like that about Drake during the internship. They'd been so young and clueless back then.

"What about you, Chaney?" Liz asked.

"Well, he does make a striking knight, but nope. Not my type."

"What is your type?" Jess asked.

"I'm not so sure anymore," Chaney admitted. "The last guy who I thought was my type let me down big-time and cost me my job."

And married my younger sister.

Drawing her brows together, Jesse frowned. "That's awful."

"It was at the time."

Tyler had gone to work for her father right before he proposed to Chaney and quickly moved up the ranks. She'd gone to work there, too, after finishing up her master's degree. But once Tyler and Simone became engaged, her parents suggested Chaney find a job at a different company. She'd gone along with the request to make them happy, even though she'd dreamed about working for her dad since she was a little girl and loved what she'd been doing.

Chaney sighed. "But that was a couple of years ago. It's over now."

Liz eyed her with curiosity. "You used to work at Dragon Llewelyn, right?"

Chaney nodded. "I did an internship there five years ago."

"Could it be you've already been rescued by the dragon knight?" Liz asked.

Chaney nearly laughed since she'd had to rescue herself from Drake back then. "No, I try to avoid having to be rescued."

"What fun is that?" Jesse kept her blue-eyed gaze locked on Drake. "Maybe we should take a fall on the grass and have Mr. Llewelyn help us up."

Oh, to be wide-eyed and naive again, believing Drake could do no wrong. No, Chaney thought, she wouldn't want to go back to that time, not for all the money in the world. "That might be a little obvious."

Liz nodded, her long bangs falling over her right eye. "Just a bit."

"I wonder if he likes girls who play hard to get," Jesse said.

"Some guys prefer a challenge," Chaney offered.

"Not Drake," Liz said. "At least not when we were taping an episode in Tuscany last year."

That tidbit of information left Chaney feeling unsettled and more curious than she had a right to be. Drake's personal business wasn't her business.

"But that taping was more of a party. Things are more proper here," Liz continued. "Still I bet there are some late-night intrigues and midnight rendezvous occurring in the castle."

Jesse sighed. "Could you imagine?"

Chaney could. In hot, living color.

She didn't want to, and downed the rest of her tea. "I'm off to refill my cup."

"Oh, oh, oh." Jesse rose up on her tiptoes. "He's coming toward us."

Liz glanced his way, but not Chaney. She wanted to keep her distance. She stared at her empty cup, wishing she hadn't left her clipboard inside. That would have given her something to concentrate on and not appear...rude.

"Hello there, Jesse. Liz. Chaney," Drake said.

When he said her name, Chaney looked at him. His gaze focused on each one of the woman, but lingered on her a moment longer than the other two.

She hated that she noticed. Or cared.

"Hi." Pink tinged Jesse's cheeks. "You were great, Mr. Llewelyn. Really, really great."

"Thank you, Jesse." He smiled at her. "Would you mind getting me a cup of tea?"

"Right away, sir." Jesse scurried toward the craft service where coffee, tea, juice, fruit and pastries had been set up for the crew.

Liz helped Drake remove his helmet. "You did excellently, sir."

Sweat dampened his hair, making him look even more attractive. "Thank you."

Liz took the helmet. "Have you ridden long?"

"A few years." He glanced at Chaney then back at Liz. "Would you please take the helmet to Russell?"

"I'd be happy to." Liz took the helmet and walked away.

"What did you think about the scene?" Drake asked Chaney.

"You nailed it." Filling in for Gemma meant giving him honest feedback even if the words would only feed his ego. "I doubt anyone could have done the scene better."

"Thank you." As he bowed his head, the wind ruffled his hair making him look oh, so tempting.

Not that she was tempted, Chaney reminded herself.

The breeze sent her hair every which way. She tucked the flying strands behind her ears.

"I've enjoyed taping the knight scenes," he said. "I'm almost sorry that was my last one in full armor."

"Halloween is coming up." She focused on his armor rather than his handsome face. "You'd be the hit at any costume party in that outfit."

"I'd need to find a willing Guinevere to accompany me."

Chaney glanced up and read the invitation in his eyes. Her mouth went dry. "Don't look at me. I don't have a costume…."

He pushed a swatch of hair off her face. The intimate gesture quickened her pulse.

"Nor are you willing," he said.

"I…" His gaze lingered on her, as if she were a prized statue to add to his collection. Still, the way he looked at her made her feel important and cherished, a way she hadn't felt in an awfully long time. She relished the moment. Of course, the adoration would never last because he'd soon find a new one to replace her with. Someone who could give him what he needed better than her. Chaney straightened.

"Sorry, no. Find somebody else to play with." Her cheeks burned. "Play your queen, I mean."

"No one else has the qualifications I'm looking for."

"You mean costume."

"I've always considered a woman's costume to be optional. Especially when we're playing." Amusement filled his eyes, as her cheeks got even hotter. "I meant no other woman is you."

"You don't even know me."

The wry grin she remembered so well from five years ago appeared. "Not for my lack of trying."

"Kissing isn't a way to get to know someone."

"It's an excellent way to start, so long as both parties are, what's the word…oh, yes, willing."

Darn him. The man could be so annoying sometimes. Strike that. All of the time. Chaney gritted her teeth. "I don't want to get into this right now."

"Later, then."

"Never." She remembered her resolve to be strong. "I'm here to help out Gemma."

"Your help is much appreciated."

"She's the only reason I'm here."

"Understood," he said. "I'd still like us to be friends."

"Friends?"

Drake nodded.

Her shoulders sagged. "You sent the flowers this morning."

Another nod.

"Thanks, they are lovely, but you didn't have to do that."

"I didn't have to, but I wanted to," he said. "What do you have to say about our being friends?"

Being friends sounded harmless enough. She appreciated he hadn't sent a dozen long-stemmed roses, yet Chaney hesitated. Drake was about as harmless as a man-eating tiger.

His watchful gaze never left hers.

Interesting. He seemed to have gained some patience over the years. He'd never liked waiting before.

"As long as being friends means things remain professional between us," she said finally.

"Professional."

"Work related," Chaney added to make sure he understood.

"Fine."

"Okay, then. We can be friends." She showed him her empty cup. "If we're finished here, I'd like to get another cup of tea."

"Before you run off, Milt wants to see you," Drake said. "He's making changes in tonight's banquet scene."

Her muscles tensed. Changes could affect the taping schedule and the budget. With his dual role, Milt seemed to like the directing more and didn't worry as much about money as most producers. That meant the budget concerns fell to the associate producer, or during this episode, her. "Do you know what kind of changes he has in mind?"

Drake's eyes gleamed with mischief. "Milt likes the period feel of the episode, so he wants extras to dress up in costume and join in on tonight's medieval feast."

She pictured the long table in the dining room and the medieval-inspired meal being prepared by the castle's chef. "Good idea. That's a big table for only one person."

"That's what Milt said."

"Except the extras will cost us."

"It's worth it."

"And the costumes—"

"The castle has them. The feast is one of their most popular requests, so they provide costumes

to make the experience more realistic for guests."
Drake glanced toward the garden where the cameraman was taping. "Russell's on it."

"That makes things easier." Though the calculator in her head still wanted to know the total expense of this scene change. "I'll go find out what Milt needs from me."

"He wants your dress size."

"My dress…" Her heart plummeted to her feet. "I can't dress up."

"Can't or won't?"

"I'm a behind-the-scenes person."

"Milt wants you at the table."

"Only Milt?" Chaney asked.

"He's in charge."

She narrowed her eyes. "You're the executive producer."

"Yes, but I had no say in this."

Drake's words made her feel only slightly better. She'd never known him not to have a say in something business related.

"You'll have fun," he added.

"Fun." She hated that word, especially coming from him. "I doubt it."

Dressing up like a medieval maiden with a dark and dangerous knight sitting next to her would not be fun. She bit her lower lip, worried.

Seeing Drake in his knight costume and looking

so gorgeous had already blurred the line between reality and fantasy. She didn't want to become a part of that confusion herself. She wanted to set professional boundaries with him. Not be wooed or courted or pulled onto his lap while a camera captured every minute of it.

"Come on," he urged. "Think about sitting at the table and eating gourmet food prepared by the castle's chef with minstrels, troubadours, jesters, mummers and jugglers to entertain you."

"Sounds crowded."

"Where's your sense of adventure?" Drake asked.

"I have no sense of adventure." She remembered how Tyler always wanted her to be something she wasn't. She'd tried, but that hadn't been good enough. "I've never been the adventurous type."

Anticipation sparkled in his eyes. "Then, my friend, we'll have to change that starting tonight."

Chaney gulped. That's what she was afraid he was going to say.

And try to do.

As the tape rolled, Drake sat at the banquet table enjoying the medieval feast with the other members of the crew and a few extras hired from a nearby village. The smell of the gourmet cuisine wafted in the air. Spices, meat, fresh-baked bread.

Smiles, lighthearted conversation and laughter surrounded him.

This was the kind of shoot he liked. No lines had to be memorized. The only direction he'd been given was to act like a knight home from war.

All he needed was a willing damsel to ravish.

One damsel in particular.

He glanced at the opposite end of the table.

Not that Drake planned on ravishing Chaney. The guilt from last night still remained. She'd made him feel like an invader about to carry her off like a spoil of war instead of a man proposing a pleasant night together. Now that she'd agreed to be friends, he wasn't about to push her and ruin everything. Especially since she seemed less tense, not as angry, this morning.

I'd prefer to keep our conversations professional. Work related.

In spite of her words, Drake believed she was more interested in him than she was willing to let on. Especially with the way her gaze kept straying to his end of the banquet table.

A minstrel strummed his lute, playing a cheerful melody.

Drake caught her looking at him again. He raised his goblet toward her and smiled.

As her cheeks reddened, she stared down at the table.

He'd bet once her fiancé took off with her sister, Chaney shut herself off from guys like a princess locked in a tower. That would explain her "hiatus." She just needed the right encouragement to unlock the door and venture outside. He was just the man—make that friend—to help her do that.

Being friends was the first step. He needed her to see him as a good guy, and a little fun was what she needed. Fun with him would follow.

Drake glanced her way again.

She looked absolutely stunning in the hunter-green-and-gold velvet gown. Brocadelike ribbons decorated the sleeves and the bodice. Her ruby necklace complemented her graceful neck and drew his gaze to her breasts, spilling out of the top of her dress.

But the way she caught a goblet as it tipped over also drew his attention. Her move was barely noticeable, so slight none of the people on her end of the table, not even the "duke" or "baron" who elbowed the glass, noticed.

Even while acting, she was still doing her job as competently as ever. If she hadn't managed the deft move, juice would have ruined one of the chef's elaborate creations and affected the taping.

Drake sipped the sparkling apple cider in his goblet. The wine and mead would arrive once the cameras stopped rolling.

A jester offered Chaney a single flower. She took the blossom with a quiet word of thanks and stuck it into the wreath of greenery she wore on top of her head. The jester broke out into a silly dance. Her glossed lips curved into a wide smile, though her dimple didn't make an appearance.

Damn. Drake lowered his goblet to the table. He couldn't tease a slight grin from her to save his life, but the village idiot dressed in colorful Harlequin plaid with bells on his hat and toes could make her smile as if he were the funniest man on Earth.

One of the extras, dressed as some sort of titled royalty, leaned over and whispered something into Chaney's ear. She nodded mysteriously. The guy smiled smugly.

A little too smugly for Drake's liking. A duel or sword fight might be a fitting end to the evening.

"Cut," Milt yelled. "Good job everyone. Take ten while the table is cleared for the next course."

"It's called a remove, not a course," someone corrected.

"Whatever," Milt said.

Drake stood. He pulled out Jesse's chair so she could stand.

She stared up at him with pure adoration. "Thank you, Mr. Llewelyn."

"Make sure you stretch your legs," he advised. "The final part of the shoot might take a while."

Jesse beamed. "I will, sir."

The intern was pretty with a fresh-faced, girl-next-door look, but so very young. Probably as young as Chaney had been when she'd interned for him, Drake realized. But Chaney had seemed...older. She'd been smart for her age, insightful and willing to voice her opinions. She'd intrigued him so much he'd been miserable her last day at the office, miserable enough that he'd broken several of his own dating rules to try and get her to stay in London longer.

Though that hadn't worked out the way he'd expected.

But he wouldn't dwell on what had happened. As his father had always told him, leave the past in the past. Chaney was here now. That was the only thing that mattered.

The extras milled about. A mummer practiced his dance steps. A juggler searched for a ball. The wait staff cleared the dishes from the table. Liz made the rounds fixing makeup and hair. Russell adjusted costumes.

Drake lost sight of Chaney in the crowded room. Three men, locals hired for the shoot and dressed in costume, stood near him.

"I really like these costumes," one said. He had been seated next to Chaney at the banquet table.

Another nodded. "I like the breasts hanging out the dresses."

The third laughed. "All we need is a costume malfunction, and I'll be a very happy man."

"All I want is a piece of that," the first one said, motioning across the room with his head.

The other glanced in that direction. "Me, too."

"I'd hit that," the third said at the same time.

Drake looked to see what woman they were talking about. He moved closer and saw all three men staring at…Chaney, her cheeks flushed and her eyes twinkling. Totally and thankfully oblivious to what was being said about her.

Anger surged through Drake's veins. He clenched his hands into fists. No one should talk about her that way. She hadn't asked to wear a revealing dress and be leered at. She was only doing her job.

Her job.

Shame hit low and hard. Drake suddenly saw how last night must have appeared in Chaney's eyes. He was so used to women falling over themselves to be with him he'd presumed he could have Chaney if he wanted her and turned on the charm.

Idiot.

Chaney deserved to be treated the way she'd asked him to treat her—professionally. With courtesy and respect, not as a sex object. And she shouldn't have needed to request that treatment from him. He should have treated her that way automatically.

As the three men made a beeline toward her, Drake cut them off and reached her first. The others backed off.

"So how is the taping going?" he asked Chaney.

"You were right." She stared up at him with clear, hazel-green eyes. "It's been a lot of fun so far."

"Perhaps there's an ounce of adventure inside of you, after all."

She brushed hair off his forehead with her fingers. "Perhaps there is."

Her soft fingertips brushed his skin. He froze, unable to breathe let alone speak.

"Though an ounce may be an exaggeration," she added.

She moved her hands lower to adjust his leather shirt.

Chaney's hands on his chest sent his heart pounding like the battle drums of the Saxons. "You don't have to keep helping me with my costumes. It was wrong of me to ask you before and I agreed to honor your request to keep things professional."

"I didn't mean…" She jerked her hands off him. Her cheeks deepened to a cherry red. "Liz and

Russell didn't think they'd have enough time during the break to get around to everyone."

His gaze took in Chaney's flushed face. She wasn't the only one embarrassed. He'd acted like a boy who had never been touched by a girl. "No worries. Nice of you to lend a hand."

"I—"

"Back in place, people," Milt ordered.

Drake could see she wanted to say something to him, but he only wanted to get away from her. His reaction had been less than professional. Still he couldn't leave her looking so confused. "We can talk later."

"Later?" she asked.

She looked so damn vulnerable he wanted to take her in his arms and hold her. Kiss her. Not exactly workplace behavior or something a friend would do.

Still he wanted to make her feel better. Drake nodded.

Her features relaxed. "Okay."

Good. She didn't look so tense. He watched her return to her seat. She was too helpful, too sweet, too beautiful. If he weren't careful…

But he was careful, especially when it came to matters of the heart. Not that his heart ever got involved or would. He knew better than to make that mistake.

Drake sat at his spot next to Jesse, keeping his eyes focused on the people sitting at his end of the banquet table. But doing so wasn't easy. His gaze wanted to stray toward Chaney.

He wouldn't allow it; he couldn't.

Everything about her unnerved him tonight, from her looks to her actions. Women never did that to Drake. At least, no woman until Chaney Sullivan.

She made him feel brutish and sexist. She brought out a rush of unfamiliar emotions like jealousy, possessiveness and protectiveness. Drake was used to being in charge, but with Chaney he didn't feel that way at all. He felt as if he were at the mercy of his emotions and all the instincts he'd honed over the years had suddenly been short-circuited.

And he didn't like it.

Forget about what happened five years ago. Forget about what he wanted to have happen with Chaney now. Being just friends would be enough, he realized. More than enough.

The sound of Chaney's laughter traveled from her end of the table smacked Drake in the gut.

Maybe even too much.

CHAPTER FOUR

TALK about sending mixed signals.

Chaney stood in front of the great hall's open fireplace, full of regret. The glowing embers of a sole log were the only remnants of tonight's banquet and the only light in the otherwise dark room.

A chill curled through her. Not from the cold, but from anticipation.

Later.

She didn't know if Drake had meant later in general terms or later as in tonight. She hoped tonight even though it was well past midnight.

Chaney wanted—no, needed—to see him. She owed Drake an apology.

What had she been thinking?

Sure, he'd looked handsome at the banquet, but he always looked good. But with the medieval costume, his beard and the mysterious smile on his face, she found herself staring at him, practically mesmerized. And as she'd feared, the line between reality and fantasy had blurred.

She crossed her arms, her fingertips brushing over the luxurious fabric of her costume.

The memory of his leather shirt and his soft hair against her fingers burned. She closed her eyes, remembering the feel of both beneath the pads of her fingertips. She'd been trying to help the stylists during the break, but for a second or two—okay, maybe longer—Chaney hadn't been one hundred percent professional. Not in her actions or her thoughts.

And she probably would have continued touching him and enjoying every second had he not said something.

Her eyes sprung open. "Idiot."

"I hope you are talking to the voices in your head again and not about someone else. Someone like me," Drake said.

She turned from the fireplace to see him striding toward her. With his long, confident gait and his costume, he looked like a king from an epic movie production. Sexy and dangerous. Larger than life.

He was an imposing figure. An attractive one, too.

Chaney wished she'd turned on a light. "I was talking about myself."

"That's a relief."

Maybe for him. Uncertainty slinked through her. "Maybe for you."

"If it's any consolation, you're not an idiot."

Not usually, but that was before seeing him again. Both her brain and memory seemed to be malfunctioning whenever he was around.

She recalled her resolve from this morning.

Unbending, unconquerable and, for the remainder of the taping, immune to Drake.

Squaring her shoulders, she crossed the room, the hem of her heavy gown brushing the tops of her feet, and met him halfway. "I want to apologize for earlier. I should have told you I was trying to help Liz and Russell before…assisting you. I'm sorry. I don't want you to think I was sending mixed signals after our talk earlier."

"No worries. I enjoyed your help," he said. "A man doesn't get fussed over by a lovely maiden every night."

His flattery heated the blood flowing through her veins. She knew he gave out compliments like candy on Halloween, but his words still pleased her. "I'm sure you have your pick of maidens."

"I'm here with the maiden of my choice."

His wide smile curled her toes. So much for being immune to him. Chaney prayed she survived tonight in one piece.

"You're still in costume," he said.

"You, too."

"I had calls to return."

"I was checking up on a few details for tomorrow." And waiting for him. She touched the large gemstone hanging around her neck. "Plus I kind of liked wearing the jewelry."

His wide smile reached his eyes sent her pulse racing. "We're all dressed up…"

"…with nowhere to go," she finished for him.

"On the contrary," he said. "Care to join me?"

Chaney narrowed her gaze suspiciously. "Where?"

"The library."

"I don't think…"

"The chef made chocolate-chip cookies. He set up a midnight snack in the library."

"Cookies," she repeated, not quite believing his invitation.

"It's all quite professional. A thank-you for the hotel staff and crew who helped with the banquet."

That included them. "A cookie does sound good."

"Let's go."

As she exited the great hall, her eyes adjusted to the light in the corridor. With Drake at her side, she could almost image them a couple from the Middle Ages. "I wonder what kings and queens walked this hallway."

"We may be able to find out when we get to the library," he said.

Chaney took in the glowing lights illuminating the tapestries and the scent of fresh-baked cookies lingering in the warm air. She breathed in the aroma. "The smell reminds me of when I was a kid. I'd get off the school bus, walk into the house and find my mom in the kitchen baking a snack."

"That must have been nice to come home to."

"It was." Now going home was more of a chore. One she did with a smile on her face and her eyes on the clock. Ever since the Tyler fiasco, Chaney's parents worried too much about her. She tried to show them she was living the perfect life so they wouldn't be concerned, even if things in her life weren't exactly perfect. "I love cookies."

"But not as much as chocolate."

She glanced his way.

"I remember," he said. "That is, I remember you like chocolate. I never knew when you and Gemma got your heads together if you were smiling over a man or a truffle."

"A truffle, no doubt." Though, in all honesty, he was probably the one who had brought a smile to their lips back then.

Drake stopped at the entrance to the library. "Our quest is over."

Chaney stepped into the dark-wood-paneled

room with its floor-to-ceiling bookcases full of hardcover books. Elegant furnishings provided seats for reading or, in their case, a place to enjoy the delicious-looking late-night snack set out on a nearby desk. In the fireplace, wood crackled as gold flames danced. The inviting fire warmed the room.

"This castle really is fairy tale worthy." She ran her fingertips along the spines of classic novels. "I feel like Belle at the moment."

"I suppose that would make me the beast."

"If the fur fits…" she teased.

Drake laughed. "Only you would admit that."

She lifted her chin and boldly met his gaze. "Arrogance and pride are common traits of a beast."

"You have me there."

"All men have a bit of a beast inside them," she said. "The question becomes how is the beast tamed?"

"Don't ask a beast that question." He strode to the cookies. "If they knew the answer, they wouldn't be so beastly."

"Perhaps, but even if the beast knew the answer, he might not do anything about it. Don't forget the beast's flaw. Arrogance. That along with his pride caused the curse. A handsome prince changed into a beast to show the world the ugliness that lies inside him, the beastly nature of his heart." Chaney joined Drake at the desk. "He had to remake himself over on the inside to win Belle's love."

"Well, I don't want Belle's love or anyone else's, so I don't have to worry about doing anything."

"Slackard."

"If the fur fits…"

She picked up one of the cookies from an ivory platter with platinum edges. "Still warm."

"Perfect timing on our parts."

Nodding, she took a bite, a delicious combination of gooey, melted chocolate and perfectly baked dough. As tasty as Drake's kiss?

Warning bells blared in her head.

Better not go there. Not even in her mind.

So what if he'd seemed to do a one-eighty from last night's flirtations. She didn't want to be attracted to Drake. He wasn't looking for love. He didn't want love. He'd just admitted that. Again. No sense being stupid about it or him.

Time to say good night. She finished her cookie, picked up a napkin and wiped her mouth.

"It's late." She'd done what she needed to do tonight—apologize. No sense sticking around any longer. Especially with a tempting beast lurking nearby. "I should call it a night, with early start tomorrow."

"Smart thinking." Drake picked up a glass. "But I'd like another cookie and a glass of milk first."

She eyed the carafe of milk sitting on ice in a silver bucket. "That does sound good."

"Stay, then," he said.

Chaney glanced around as if someone would magically appear to give her permission or tell her to leave. No one did. She probably shouldn't stay, but, heaven help her, she wanted to. "I will for a few minutes."

He handed her a glass. "Nothing beats milk and cookies."

She sat on a love seat. "When was the last time you had cookies and milk?"

"Three weeks ago." He set a small plate with a few cookies on it within arm's reach of the sofa and sat next to her. "With my father."

Drake's nearness disturbed her, as did his thigh touching hers. Her skin practically burned in spite of the layers of clothing between them. She tried not to think about it, about him. "Do you see your father often?"

"It depends on my schedule," Drake said. "But I try to see him as much as possible."

That was more than she could say of herself.

Chaney didn't live that far from her parents, but her parents' worry seemed to be in direct proportion to the amount of free time she had on her hands. The busier she was, the happier they seemed, so she stayed away from them, even if it meant spending a lonely evening in her apartment instead of being with family.

"This weekend, we're heading to Scotland to celebrate his birthday." Drake sipped his milk. "Golf has become his passion so I know he will beat me handily every round."

The affection in Drake's tone, his soft inflection, hinted at a deeper side of the billionaire playboy, a side she hadn't known existed. "I'm sure he's the one person you don't mind losing to."

"He's the only one I will gladly lose to," Drake said. "To tell you the truth, I've been looking forward to the holiday for weeks, as has my dad."

"The flight you need to catch tomorrow—" she reached for a cookie off the small plate "—is that to Scotland?"

He nodded. "My father is meeting me at Heathrow."

"Now I know why Gemma said the taping must end on time." And why they had hired locals to fill out the crew.

Another nod. "It'll take an act of God for me to miss that flight. I don't want to disappoint my dad."

"I'll make sure you don't."

"Thank you."

"You're welcome." This new side of Drake intrigued her. She wanted to know more about him. "What about your mom?"

Drake's eyes darkened to a dark chocolate brown. "My mother left when I was two years old. I never saw her again."

The thought of a two-year-old being deserted by his mother was unimaginable. Chaney's heart ached for him. She fought the urge to comfort him, but gave in and touched his forearm. Through the fabric she felt his muscles bunch beneath her palm. "I'm so sorry, Drake."

The sentiment seemed so trite, but she didn't know what else to say. She dragged her hand and away from him and placed it on her lap.

Drake shrugged, but his mouth tightened. "Don't be sorry. She had different priorities."

He sounded almost indifferent about the situation. "That's not something a child would understand."

The intensity of his gaze took her breath away.

"No, but I understand now," he said. "I know how hard it was for my dad to raise me on his own. I owe him…everything."

"He must be so proud of you."

A satisfied smile settled on Drake's lips. "He is."

The gratitude in his voice sent the warm and fuzzies shooting through Chaney. Uh-oh. This was the man she'd fantasized about five years ago. Family oriented, generous, a gentleman. This was the kind of man she wanted to fall in love with someday. Yet this was only one part of Drake

Llewelyn. She knew the other part all too well—flirt, player and rake.

Still she couldn't take her gaze off him.

She sipped her milk, but barely tasted the cold liquid. She could have been drinking cough syrup. All her attention was focused on him.

"I've told you about my father." Drake placed his hand on the back of the sofa, not quite around her, but close enough to send her leaning away from him. "So far I know your mother bakes. You told me years ago your father owns his own financial company. Tell me about your sister."

"Simone is three years younger than me," Chaney said. "She was named after an actress, Simone Simon."

"Let me guess, a horror actress."

"She starred in the movie *Cat People*."

Drake laughed.

"Simone and I are total opposites. In high school, I was president of the National Honor Society. She was the head cheerleader," Chaney said. "We never got along because we had nothing in common. Simone is very competitive. I'm not. But there's always been an odd competitiveness between us, from the time we were little. It's something I never understood. I still don't."

"Some people are more competitive than others."

Chaney nodded. "It's all about winning for Simone. Coming out ahead."

"There's nothing wrong with wanting to win," he said. "I play to win."

"I'd rather not even take part in the game."

"You can't win if you don't play."

"You can't lose if you don't play."

"What do you have to lose?" Drake asked.

Her self-respect. Her heart. Chaney shrugged. "I guess I've already lost it all, and I'd rather not go through that again."

"Not everyone is like your sister. It's not necessary to hurt people to win."

Chaney reached for another cookie. More chocolate sounded good right now. "I've probably painted a very negative image of my sister."

"She's done that for herself."

"Simone does love Tyler," Chaney said. "Way more than I ever did."

"Yet you agreed to marry him."

She heard the question in his voice and tried to decide how to reply. She'd returned from her internship in London disillusioned about love after Drake had propositioned her. She'd wanted to prove she wasn't a bad judge of men. She'd wanted to prove to herself Mr. Right existed. And find him.

"I guess I was ready to fall in love," she admitted. "Tyler seemed like a safe choice at the time."

"The safest choice to fit your long-range investment goals."

"Something like that." Chaney hadn't wanted to be disappointed in love, and Tyler seemed like a sure bet. Though in retrospect, she probably would have been better off staying in London with Drake, even if that had never gone anywhere except his bedroom. At least he'd been honest about what he wanted from her. "My pride was bruised, but everything worked out for the best. He wasn't my true love."

"You sound certain."

"I am," she said with confidence. "My true love would never have looked twice at my sister, let alone dumped me for her."

"Touché." Drake's assessing gaze pierced right through her, and made her shift positions on the couch. "But that kind of betrayal had to have hurt."

"Yes, but what was I going to do? Choose not to be a part of my family any longer? I couldn't do that to my parents. They were torn up about it enough. They couldn't pick one daughter over another. Me throwing a hissy fit would only make my parents feel worse, so I sucked it up, agreed to be Simone's maid of honor and the rest is history."

Doormats R Us. She ate a bite of her cookie.

"You're something else, Chaney Sullivan."

The way he looked at her with what seemed like

pride made her sit taller. She raised her chin. "I'll take that as a compliment."

"You should."

Good, because she wanted to.

Being here with Drake felt more like a date than two friends sharing a late night snack. She almost wished it were a date. There seemed to be a connection between them, one that kept getting stronger the more time she spent with him.

That worried her.

Having others join them might not be such a bad thing. Chaney glanced at the entrance to the library, hoping to catch someone out in the hallway and invite them in. No one passed by. "It's so quiet. I wonder where everyone else is?"

"The chef said he was setting out cookies in the solarium, too," Drake explained. "Maybe that's where the others are."

She took another sip of her milk, wishing the others would swing by the library on their way to their rooms.

"I have to admit," he said. "I'm enjoying having you to myself and getting to know you better."

"Me, too." Except, now that she'd gotten to see a different side to him, Chaney wanted to know a whole lot more about Drake. Questions swirled through her mind.

Who else besides his father does he make time

to see? How much did his mother's leaving affect Drake's views on relationships? Would he ever change his mind about making a commitment to a woman he loved?

But even though Chaney wanted to know the answers, she didn't dare ask the questions.

She needed to stick to her resolve where Drake was concerned. He was not only trouble with a capital *T,* but also temptation. Both, she'd learned the hard way, were to be avoided at all costs.

And that made it clear what she needed to do right now…

Say good-night.

On Sunday morning a dim light filtered into the room through the open curtains. Drake rose up on his elbows and stared out the arched window. The dark skies matched the storm brewing inside him.

He hadn't slept well. Okay, he hadn't slept much, if at all. The reason—Chaney Sullivan.

In less than twenty-four hours, she'd wormed her way under his skin. Something no other woman had managed to do in a very long time. If ever.

Just friends, Drake reminded himself.

Still he couldn't stop thinking about her. She captivated him. He wanted to see her again. This morning if possible.

He couldn't believe another man hadn't already snatched her up.

Not that he himself would.

Drake wasn't interested in having a relationship. He didn't want a girlfriend. A woman like Chaney wouldn't settle for any less.

"Well, I don't plan on settling down anytime soon," she'd said.

But she wanted to settle down someday.

"I do believe true love exists."

That told Drake all he needed to know.

A relationship with Chaney would never work out. They held opposite views about love. Not that he was looking for love or even a serious girlfriend.

No way would he ever let a woman get close enough to hurt him the way his mother destroyed his father. And the last thing Drake would ever want to do was hurt Chaney the way others in her life had.

Best to stay goodbye and be done with it. Her. All he had to do was make it through today. Avoiding her seemed like his best bet.

As the day progressed, Drake didn't have to worry about seeing Chaney. She was too busy putting out fires on the set.

A blown fuse had delayed taping, and she worked hard to get everything fixed and back on schedule. The taping even finished early. She'd done her job beautifully, never allowing the relaxed atmosphere to become tense or anxious. Drake couldn't help but be impressed. And though his helicopter was waiting, he wanted to thank Chaney for her hard work.

He strode through drizzling rain to the production office, a meeting room inside the castle. He found her sitting on her knees packing up a fax machine.

Seeing her filled him with warmth despite his damp hair and clothing. The sooner he said goodbye, the better.

"Chaney," he said.

She glanced up at him. "Don't you have a helicopter to catch?"

"In a few minutes, but I wanted to say thank you before I left."

"You're welcome. I'm glad I could help out." Her smile made his heart stumble over the next beat. "You're all wet."

"The rain."

"You English and your rain," she teased. "Be careful you don't catch a cold. That would ruin your golf vacation."

Drake couldn't care less about his holiday at the moment—the clearest sign he should leave now. But his feet remained firmly planted in place, as if cemented to the floor.

Getting out of there might be the smartest move,

but he wasn't ready to walk away just yet. "I have clothes to change into."

The phone rang. She glanced at the handset. Her smile widened. "It's Gemma. No doubt checking up on me."

Chaney answered the phone. "Hey, no need to worry. We finished taping forty minutes ago."

A moment passed. And another.

Her smile vanished. Her face paled. "Oh, Gemma."

The anguish in Chaney's voice knotted Drake's stomach. "Is everything all right?" he whispered.

She shook her head.

He took a step toward her.

"Drake is right here, Gemma." Chaney hit a button and returned the receiver to the cradle. "You're on speaker phone."

"Hello, Gem." Drake tried to sound calm and unconcerned. "Tell me what's going on."

"I had an ultrasound at my doctor's appointment." Gemma's voice cracked. "I thought they'd be taking me off bed rest, but they saw…they saw that the placenta is separating."

Drake had no idea what that meant, but it didn't sound good. He looked at a worried Chaney. "The baby…"

"The baby is fine." Gemma sniffled. "At least right now."

Relief hit him. "Good."

"I know it won't be easy, but you need to try not to worry," Chaney said.

"I've been restricted to bed rest for the remainder of the pregnancy." Gemma sounded as if she had been crying. "I'm so sorry, Drake. There are all those episodes left to tape and plans for the next season—"

"Stop, Gem," he ordered, his voice firm. "The only thing that matters is you and the baby."

"Listen to Drake," Chaney said without a moment's hesitation, and he appreciated her backing him up. "The show might need you, but your baby needs you more."

"But I hate leaving you and the show in the lurch, Drake." Emotion filled Gemma's already strained voice. "You've done so much for me and Oliver."

"We'll muddle through."

"That's exactly what they'll do." Chaney sounded encouraging. "Don't worry about it, Gemma. Focus on you and the baby."

"I wouldn't worry so much if I knew things would be covered, Drake," Gemma said. "Otherwise, it might impact your golf holiday with your dad."

Drake hadn't even considered that, but Gemma was right. Guest hosts, ones they'd never used before, were scheduled to host the remaining episodes. If he were hosting, they could get by without an associate producer, but problems sometimes cropped up with new hosts. Milt could only do so much on his own. "You and the baby take precedent over my holiday, Gem. My father will understand if I have to cancel."

As he always had in the past.

"But if Chaney could stay on…" Gemma suggested.

"That's a brilliant suggestion." Drake smiled. Chaney was the perfect solution to his dilemma, since she knew what needed to be done and got along well with the crew. And he wouldn't have to interact with her, as he'd be in Scotland on holiday. He looked at her. "I would appreciate it if you could continue on. I won't be at the tapings and need someone I trust to oversee things."

Lines creased Chaney's forehead. "I would be happy to help you out, but I need to talk to my boss before I can commit to anything."

"But if he said yes?" Gemma asked.

"I could stay on for as long as he allowed me to." Chaney no doubt heard the hope returning to Gemma's voice and didn't want that to disappear.

"I hope he says yes," Gemma said. "I can bring you up to speed on things."

"Don't even think about work," Drake ordered.

"Talking to Chaney won't be like work,"

Gemma countered, "more like chatting like old times. Call me once you talk to your boss."

"Will do," Chaney said.

"Oliver's here with a cup of tea and a scone. I'd better hang up."

"Make sure that husband of yours keeps spoiling you," Chaney said.

"Stay off your feet and follow your doctor's orders," Drake added. "I'll ring you from Scotland."

"On your holiday no less." Gemma's suddenly lighthearted tone brought a smile to his face. "You are the best boss in the world."

"I know," Drake said. "Goodbye, Gem."

"Bye."

The call disconnected.

He stared at Chaney. Concern clouded her hazel-green eyes. "You made her feel better. Thank you."

"I'm relieved she feels better, but I hope you don't feel roped into keeping me on. I understand if you'd rather find someone with more experience."

"After seeing you in action here, I know you have what it takes for the job. But I don't want you feeling as if I'm dumping this all on you," he said. "I can delay my holiday if you'd rather return home."

"You can't delay your trip." Two lines formed above the bridge of her nose. "It's your father's birthday. That wouldn't be right."

"It's happened before."

"That's one time too many," she said. "But I've got to warn you, I don't have any vacation left. My boss will have to agree to a leave of absence without pay."

"Let's hope he agrees," Drake said. "And I'll see you're well compensated for your time."

"Thanks, but this is really about helping Gemma."

He remembered what Chaney had said to him on Friday: "I'm only here as a favor for Gemma."

That was as clear as Baccarat crystal now. Drake almost laughed at his own arrogance and pride. The attraction was one sided. His side. He'd wanted to avoid her, but he needn't worry about Chaney Sullivan.

She might have gotten under his skin, but she hadn't meant to do it. She wasn't after his heart or him. She only wanted to help Gemma.

All he had to do was control his attraction to her, and everything would work out fine.

She stared at the phone. "It's too early to call L.A., but I really hope my boss says yes so I can stay."

The longing in her voice reaffirmed her reasons for wanting to stay—to help out a friend. Her staying appealed to him, too.

She was in the position to help not only Gem, but also him and the show. He made a practice of acquiring attractive assets when they became available. The two things made for a sound business decision.

"If he doesn't let you take a leave of absence," Drake explained. "There's always another option."

"What's that?"

"You could quit."

Chaney narrowed her eyes. "Why would I quit my job?"

"So you could take a permanent position at the Dragon Channel," Drake said.

"You would hire me full time?"

"Yes," he said without a doubt. "You proved yourself during your internship and then again here during the taping. You are intelligent, conscientious and hardworking. You've got a strong character and work ethic. You'd be a perfect fit for Dragon Llewelyn."

And, he realized, for him.

If, Drake qualified with a big *if,* he was interested in pursuing a relationship. Which he wasn't.

He stared at her earnest eyes and her pretty smile.

Not the least bit interested.

You'd be a perfect fit for Dragon Llewelyn.

Chaney sighed. But not, it seemed, for Drake Llewelyn.

Since arriving at the underwater resort on a

small island in the South Pacific two days ago, she hadn't heard a word from her new boss. Granted, he was on vacation, but a little interest from him would have been well, nice. Instead she was stuck with their guest talent, Foster Smalley, a fifty-something billionaire with perfectly tanned skin, a diamond stud earring and a buff body he liked to show off.

She really missed Drake.

Prima donna didn't begin to describe Foster. Obsessively compulsive about working out, he demanded additional equipment be brought in to the resort's fully equipped gym. He would only drink mineral water bottled in glass, something not easy to find on a remote island. He required giving his approval on all footage he appeared on. And now…

"The temperature is too cold." Foster stared down his nose at Milt. "I could become hypothermic. Putting my health at risk wasn't in the contract."

"It's a hot tub. Emphasis on hot." Milt rubbed the back of his neck, no doubt trying to ward off another headache. The entire crew had been having them ever since Foster arrived. "There's no way you'll come close to hypothermia."

"That water is too cold." Foster expected everyone to cater to his every desire, no matter how petty. And they'd tried. Within reason and their budget. "I'm not taping this scene."

Milt drew in a long breath. The tense lines around his mouth made him look as if he wanted to punch something. Or someone.

Chaney knew exactly how he felt. She couldn't believe someone like this would have actually offered to be a guest host. Maybe he wanted to get back at Drake for something. Or maybe Foster was just a rude jerk.

She could handle the temperamental talent. That was what Drake hired her for. What he wanted her for. All he wanted her for.

All she wanted was to stop the random thoughts of him that kept popping into her mind. Soon, she hoped. Very soon. But right now she had her producer to rescue. She squared her shoulders.

"Hey, Foster." Chaney pasted on her sweetest smile. "While Milt looks at some different scenarios for the next scene, why don't you and I see what we can come up with ourselves?"

"Work on your mind, son?" Rhys Llewelyn asked.

Not work. Chaney.

Standing at the seventh hole, Drake realized he'd been staring at his bag of clubs for a long time. He pulled out his eight iron. "I was wondering how the taping was going. They should have finished up at the underwater resort and moved on to Patagonia by now."

His father studied the greens. "Give them a call."

Drake had every confidence in Chaney's ability to handle the taping. That was what he'd hired her for.

All he'd hired her for.

Good executives learned to delegate responsibility. He placed his ball on the tee and took a practice swing. The iron swooshed through the air.

But he had to admit he was…curious. "If there were any big problems, I would have heard something."

"You would rather be there," Rhys said.

He would, Drake realized. "It's not that, Dad. I have a new associate producer."

"And you don't think he can handle the job."

"She." He took another practice swing. "I'm sure she's doing a fine job. She's very competent."

Rhys's curious gaze met Drake's. "Pretty?"

"That, too," he admitted.

His father grinned. "No wonder you can't keep your mind on your game."

Drake frowned. He didn't like the idea of a woman distracting him. He'd created a perfect fantasy that kept her front and center in his mind. Maybe he needed to deal with Chaney in a different way.

Instead of denying or ignoring his attraction, he should explore it. Once he did that, he could get her out of his system once and for all. Her appeal had to be about the challenge she posed. The not knowing. The mystery.

"Stop thinking about work, and you'll play better," Rhys said.

Once Drake proved there wasn't anything between him and Chaney except some physical chemistry, he'd be back on his game.

He swung his iron and sent the ball soaring into the air, a white dot against the steely gray sky. The ball landed on the green and rolled eight feet from the hole.

Rhys patted him on the back. "Outstanding shot."

Now all Drake needed was a shot at Chaney.

CHAPTER FIVE

CHANEY sat in Gemma's living room. On the table was breakfast: scones, clotted cream, fruit and tea. "The last two weeks have been such a blur. London, L.A., the South Pacific, Patagonia. The jet lag is killing me. How did you do it?"

"It's bad at first." Gemma lay on the couch. "You eventually get used to the travel and odd hours. Drake does go out of his way to make things easier and fun, but the pregnancy made it harder. I was always tired."

"Well, better me than you," Chaney said. "This is exactly the experience my boss said I needed if I wanted that promotion."

Gemma added sugar to her teacup. "I'm sure you'll get the job now."

"When I turned in my application, my boss said the hands-on production experience with *The Billionaire's Playground* would make me a strongly qualified applicant," she admitted. "Of course to get the time off to gain that experience, I worked two eighteen-hour days to finish everything in my in-box so my leave wouldn't impact the department. But it was worth it. Not only did I get to work on two more episodes, I get to see you again."

"The best part," Gemma said.

"Sure is." Chaney bit into a buttered scone. The pastry melted in her mouth and probably added an inch to her thighs. She didn't care. "I haven't found scones like these at home."

Gemma patted her round belly. "I hope you'll come back after this little one is born and have more."

"You know I will." Chaney glanced at the clock. "I wish I could stay longer now, but need to get to the office. A talent issue wreaked havoc with the budget, and I'm taking Milt's place at a meeting."

"Don't be worried. You'll do great," Gemma said. "Have a safe flight home tomorrow."

Chaney leaned over and hugged her friend. "Take care of yourself and the little one in your tummy."

An hour later she sat in a meeting room at a table with Drake and two bigwigs from the Dragon Channel whom she nicknamed salt and pepper. Zander, a man with white hair, who couldn't have been older than forty, and Angelica, a thirty-something woman with long, jet-black

hair, who looked more like an actress with her
exotic looks than a television executive. The three
spoke about ratings, ad revenue and next season
of *The Billionaire's Playground.*

Chaney added her input as required, but she
wished Milt hadn't asked her to step in for him. Yes,
she understood his frustration over what happened
during the two tapings, but being here with Drake
was messing with how they'd left things at the castle,
namely: keep things professional and just be friends.

He was definitely the most gorgeous male
friend she'd ever had.

He still had his beard, but a tailored suit, dress
shirt and silk tie replaced his armor. Even dressed
like a billionaire businessman, he had an edge to
him. A dark, dangerous, sexy edge.

Now Chaney was the frustrated one. She took
a sip of her lukewarm tea.

Not only did he look hot, seeing Drake in action
during the meeting had increased her attraction for
him. The way he answered questions, relying only
on the facts and figures stored in his brain, amazed
her. He never once referred to notes or a computer.

She forced herself not to stare and concentrated
on the financial statement in front of her.

"Was the talent a pain in the ass, Chaney?"
Zander asked.

"He was more of an ass actually," she admitted.

Everyone laughed.

Drake ran his fingers over his beard. "I heard you handled him well, Chaney."

His compliment pleased her. "I tried."

"What happened?" Angelica asked.

"The host talent's demands were excessive and expensive as were his wife's. At least, I think she was his wife. We were never formerly introduced," Chaney explained. "Even the simplest stand-up took hours to tape due to his constant tantrums. We were more prepared in Patagonia, but he was still a problem. I've documented everything in the episode summaries. You may want to rethink using him again."

"He won't be hosting another episode," Drake said. "I've decided to host the final episode of season so we don't run into this same problem."

His gaze met hers, then he looked away.

Darn. Drake might have enjoyed his golfing holiday, but now he would have to clean up her mess. It was a good thing she was flying home tomorrow. She'd done what she could but it hadn't been enough. She'd disappointed Drake and let down Gemma. "I'm sorry."

"It's not your fault," Drake said. "I'd been thinking of hosting the last episode, anyway."

"That's true," Zander said. "But no one thought you would be able to fit it in."

"I switched a few things in my calendar." Drake picked up a pen from the table and twirled it with his fingers. "It's not a problem."

Not for her. Chaney would be back to work at the studio while they taped the final episode, a world away from a private island in the Bahamas where they would tape next. That was a good thing because she wanted to put distance between her and Drake so she could forget about him. He'd been on her mind too much the last two weeks.

"The advertisers will be pleased," Angelica said. "You bring in higher ratings."

Chaney nodded.

"Is there anything else?" Zander asked. "We have another meeting to get to."

"We've covered everything we needed to here," Drake said. "Thanks."

As the others gathered their things, Chaney stood. She still had a few pieces of paperwork to fill out and turn in. Besides, with the way her attraction had grown exponentially during the meeting, the last thing she wanted was to be alone with Drake, even in a glass-walled room that reminded her of a fish tank on steroids.

"Wait, Chaney." The way he said her name sent a bevy of butterflies flapping. "I want to speak with you for a minute."

Her stomach knotted. That buttery scone

she'd eaten at Chaney's suddenly seemed like a very bad idea.

While Drake walked the other two people out, she sat and reviewed the notes she'd taken during the meeting. The writing on her notepad blurred. She refocused but had to read one sentence three times to make sense of the words.

Drake sat next to her.

She tried not to notice the way he smelled. She toyed one of the corners of her notepad, nervous what he might say.

"Don't blame yourself for the budget overruns. I meant what I said. You did an excellent job on the episodes," Drake said. "Everyone is impressed with your work. Milt said it would have been worse if you hadn't stepped in."

Her tight shoulders relaxed a little. "I was only doing my job, but I don't think I endeared myself to our guest host."

"You did what needed to be done," Drake said. "And endeared yourself to not only the production crew, but the Dragon Channel."

She stifled a yawn. "Thank you."

"You look tired."

"I am a little jet-lagged."

"You get used to the travel after a while."

"Well, I won't need to get used to it," she admitted.

"That's right," he said. "You're heading home tomorrow."

She nodded. "I plan on sleeping the entire eleven-hour flight."

"You'll need a nap today to be ready for tonight."

"Tonight?" she asked.

"Gem's surprise party. That's what I wanted to talk to you about."

Chaney stared at him confused. She was tired, but not that tired. "Gemma's birthday was two months ago."

"Oliver and I thought a little party might cheer her up. She loves getting together with people."

"That's thoughtful of you, but don't you think it might overwhelm her?"

"Gem doesn't have to do anything. Neither does Oliver," Drake said. "I hired an event planner to take care of all the details. It's just going to be a small Halloween party."

So much for going to bed early. "It'll be nice to spend more time with Gemma. Plus I can't wait to see her reaction to your surprise."

"I'll pick you up at your hotel," he offered.

Chaney tensed. "That's not necessary. You're going to enough trouble with the party."

"Your hotel is on the way."

A ride would be better than having to take the

Tube, given how tired she was. Turning him down would be plain stupid.

"Okay," Chaney said. "Thanks."

"I'll take care of everything." His watchful gaze studied her, clouded with concern. "Go back to your hotel and sleep."

"I have to finish up a few things here, then I will."

"You'd better."

The concern in his voice sent a rush of warmth flowing through her. She knew he concern was strictly professional, but she liked it. More than she probably should.

"I'll be by at five-thirty to pick you up," he said. "We'll spring the surprise on Gem so the event planner can get everything set up and ready before the other guests arrive."

The thought of seeing him again so soon curved Chaney's lips, then she remembered she wanted distance. But distance would keep her from Gemma's party. That wouldn't be good.

Tonight wasn't about Drake. It was for her longtime friend and former roommate.

"I'll be ready and more awake by then," Chaney said. "I won't let Gemma down."

Or, Chaney thought, herself.

Drake stood in front of the door to Chaney's hotel room, anxious about tonight.

About her.

She was smart, hardworking and beautiful. This was his chance to prove nothing but physical attraction existed between them. Spending this final night with Chaney would get her off his mind and out of his life forever. He could close this chapter and forget about it. Forget about her.

The gold number on the door, 323, shone against the ivory-colored paint. The small boutique hotel was a favorite among visiting employees. It boasted an attentive staff, nicely appointed rooms and was within walking distance of both the office and a Tube station. He liked the place because he could walk through the lobby dressed like a knight from the round table and not be stared at or even noticed.

He held the garment bag containing Chaney's costume in one hand and knocked on the door with the other. The sound cracked the silence in the empty hallway like a gunshot at dawn.

He shifted his weight between his feet.

The door opened. Chaney, looking pretty in a pair of black pants and a pink tunic, stared at him. She'd pulled her hair back into a loose ponytail. Those sexy smart-girl glasses of hers were nowhere in sight, so he assumed she was wearing contacts. The nap must have reenergized her.

Chaney's brow furrowed. "Why are you wearing your knight costume?"

"It's a Halloween Party. Those usually require fancy dress."

"So that's why you kept your beard."

"Yes, and the ladies seem to like it, too."

Her mouth quirked. "I'm sure they do."

"You don't like the beard."

"I didn't say that," she said. "Normally I don't like facial hair, but on you…"

The way she studied him made him feel like a piece of meat on display in the butcher's case.

"Go on," he urged.

"The beard works," she said finally.

Drake didn't know why her words made him feel so relieved.

"But we have a problem," she continued. "When you said Halloween party, I didn't even think about needing a costume. I guess I was more tired than I realized."

"Never fear, my lady. I told you I would take care of everything and I have." Drake handed her the garment bag. "Your costume."

"Thank you." She eyed the bag warily as if it contained a poisonous snake instead of clothing. "So what am I going to be?"

"Try the costume on, and you'll see."

"Okay, thanks." Chaney opened the door to her room and motioned Drake into the room. "I can change in the bathroom."

He walked inside and closed the door behind him.

"I'll be quick," she said.

"We've got forty-five minutes until we meet the event planner outside of Gemma's house," he said. "The party doesn't start until eight."

Chaney disappeared into the bathroom.

Drake heard the sound of a zipper. Her pants. He wondered if she'd unbuttoned her blouse. The thought of her undressing sent his temperature up.

Seeking a distraction, he stepped away from the bathroom door. He noticed her laptop, a travel book on Patagonia, where the last episode had been taped, and the notebook she'd had at the meeting earlier. Her pens, three of them, lay in a neat row, all with caps on. He wondered if her office was so tidy and organized. And her home.

The only thing not in perfect order was her bed.

Drake walked toward the bed and touched the indention on the pillowcase where her head must have lain during her nap. He imagined the silky strands of her hair spread out over the white linen.

Over him.

His temperature spiraled. He knew he couldn't blame it on the armor. So much for this distraction.

He focused on the nightstand next to the bed instead. A lamp, the phone, a digital clock and a small silver-framed photograph of a family with a large dog.

The picture drew his attention. Chaney looked like a teenager, her no-longer-present dimple very apparent in this photograph. He guessed the other young woman must be her sister. She was shorter than Chaney with blond hair and her chest pushed out to emphasize her breasts. The women stood on either side of the dog—a German shepherd, if he wasn't mistaken—and two smiling adults who must be her horror-movie-loving parents.

The bathroom door opened.

He returned the frame to its place and stepped into the center of the room.

Chaney walked out, wearing an emerald gown that brought out the green in her eyes. The low neckline showed off her breasts. The tight bodice accentuated her narrow waist. She'd taken out the ponytail and wore her hair lose with a headpiece. She looked like a…queen.

He sucked in a breath. Stunning.

"Guinevere." She placed her hands on her hips. "You brought me a Guinevere costume to wear."

He laughed at her outrage. "I told you at the castle if I was going to be Lancelot I needed a Guinevere to accompany me."

"If I remember correctly, you wanted a willing Guinevere."

"You're so unwilling you would disappoint

your friend by not dressing up when you have a costume?"

"Of course not, but I thought you were giving me a ride to the party, not having us attend as Guinevere and Lancelot. People may…talk."

"I'm used to people talking about me."

"Unfortunately, I am, too, but not in a work situation."

"It's your last night in town," he said. "Your reputation is safe."

"It's not mine I'm worried about."

Her concern over him surprised him. "I appreciate the thought, but I will be fine."

Her mouth thinned. "Do you always get your way?"

"Usually."

A flash of annoyance crossed her face. "I figured as much."

"In my defense, only you would do as Guinevere."

She pursed her glossed lips. "I find that hard to believe."

"It's true." She was the only woman he wanted to be with right now. "Be my queen tonight."

Drake recognized her hesitation. Tomorrow she could do whatever she wanted, but tonight he wasn't going to let her get away from him.

"Do it for Gem," he urged.

A beat passed. And another. Something—loyalty, perhaps— flickered in her eyes. Drake knew he had her.

"For Gemma," Chaney said finally.

"Thank you." He bowed. "In return, I shall be your protector tonight."

"No, I will be yours," she countered. "You'll need someone to protect you from all the women at the party who will want to see what you've got on under all that shining armor."

He grinned, enjoying this. Her.

He played to win. He wasn't about to lose tonight. "You're welcome to borrow my sword if you need it."

"Thank you, sire." She curtsied. "I'll do whatever it takes to ensure your safety and your virtue."

Then she'd better stay far, far away from him. She was too lovely for his own good. But given she was leaving the country tomorrow he needn't worry.

He extended his arm. "Our transport awaits us, my lady."

She grabbed her purse. "Transport?"

"My limo."

She shook her head and linked her arm with his. "Why do I have a feeling tonight's going to be like an episode of *The Billionaire's Playground*?"

"Perhaps because I'm a billionaire and London is one of my playgrounds."

She gave him a look. "How many times have you used that line before?"

He grinned. "It looks like one time too many."

She laughed. "Let's go surprise Gemma."

Drake sure knew who to call when throwing a party.

Outside Gemma's house, Chaney found an army of people—the event planner, caterers, florist, servers, bartenders, even a D.J. "If all these people are needed to put on a small gathering, I can't imagine what your idea of a full-blown party would look like."

He grinned. "I may have gone a tad overboard tonight."

She looked around at what was waiting to be carried into Gemma's modest house. Two burly looking men stood next to a gold Cleopatra-style chaise.

"You think?" Chaney teased. "That knight costume of yours sure fits your deeds tonight."

Drake bowed and led her to the front door. Oliver answered. The three of them went into the living room where Gemma lay, and yelled, "Surprise."

The next forty-five minutes sped by.

Chaney helped Gemma put on a Cleopatra costume and wig. Oliver situated the mother-to-be on her throne, the gold chaise, which was the only furniture except for chairs remaining in the living room.

The burly guys must have been busy. Everyone had been.

The scent of delicious food drifted out from the kitchen. A buffet had been set up on the dining room table. A dj set up his equipment and even put down a temporary dance floor.

Gemma, wearing a white Egyptian gown, a gold collar and black wig and thick eyeliner, stared at how her house had been transformed into party central. "I can't believe all this."

"Believe it," Drake said. "And enjoy."

Chaney knew he cared about his employees, but this party seemed to go beyond what a normal boss would do for an employee. She didn't get it or him. Still she appreciated what he'd done and the smile he'd put on Gemma's face.

Less than an hour later, the party was in full swing.

Waiters carried trays of hot appetizers and Halloween-themed drinks. The dj played dance songs, including the "Monster Mash" and "Thriller," and whatever else anyone requested. The top-notch dessert buffet in the dining room was a huge hit.

Gemma beamed from her chaise. "You really are the best boss in the world, Drake."

He winked. "Told you so."

"He told me so, too." Oliver, dressed as Marc Antony, held his wife's hand and gazed lovingly into her eyes. "I wasn't sure about this at first, but Drake was right about it bringing your smile back."

Oliver kissed Gemma.

Seeing her friend with her adoring husband brought a taffy-size lump to Chaney's throat. She couldn't believe how much the two loved each other. She hadn't ever felt that way about anyone, not even Tyler. She hoped would would. Someday.

Her gaze strayed to Drake.

Once upon a time she'd wanted him to be the love of her life. She'd been so young then, full of daydreams and unrealistic expectations. But seeing him look so handsome and noble in the knight costume made her almost believe Drake could still be it.

He looked at her with an odd expression on his face.

Embarrassed to be caught staring, she picked up Gemma's empty glass. "I'll refill this with the sparkling cider."

Time flew. The food and drink overflowed. Music played. People in costumes danced.

From her throne in the living room, the mother-to-be glowed. Gemma wasn't quite her old self, but closer than she'd been in a while. Chaney wouldn't have wanted to miss tonight for the world. And Drake was the one to thank for that.

Drake.

Chaney had lost track of him. She searched the kitchen and dining room. A mummy, a construction worker, a French maid, but no knight. She glanced around the crowded living room. Something shiny and silver caught her eye. She took a closer look. Definitely armor and…

Uh-oh. Three women surrounded him, hungry-looking women. One, a brunette, showed all her "assets" in a playboy bunny suit. Another, a blonde, wore a pirate costume that left little to the imagination. The third, a redhead, had a black cape around her shoulders, a leather corset, fishnet stockings and vampire teeth in her mouth that were as sharp as her stiletto heels. All three looked as if they wanted to take a bite of Drake.

An unfamiliar possessiveness grabbed hold of Chaney. She might not be his official date, but they'd come as Lancelot and Guinevere. Chaney had also said she would be his queen tonight and promised to protect him.

Time to put her words into action.

Squaring her shoulders, she walked toward Drake. The flow of the gown made her feel strong, powerful, as if she were the legendary queen with the two bravest, hottest men in the kingdom in love with her.

"Excuse me, ladies—" she laced her fingers with Drake's, not easy to do with him wearing gauntlets "—but the dj is going to be playing our song next."

If looks could kill, Chaney would be a goner.

She didn't care.

Not with the pleased smile lighting up Drake's face.

Confidence shot through her. She pulled him onto the makeshift dance floor, joining a handful of other couples out there.

His warm gaze met hers. "A little possessive tonight, darling."

"Not possessive—" she faced him "—protective."

The faster rock beat gave way to another song. A slow song.

As his smile crinkled the corners of his eyes, he held her right hand with his left and assumed a dance position.

She stood in between his feet, careful not to touch his thighs with her legs, feeling an odd mix of embarrassment and pleasure.

His right hand rested on her hip. "Some might call it territorial."

"A queen's prerogative." She placed her left hand on his shoulder, the armor hard beneath her palm. "Would you rather I send you back to the piranhas?"

"I'd rather dance to our song. What song is it?"

She listened to the music. "'Can't Help Falling in Love' by Elvis Presley."

"A good thing the song wasn't 'Hound Dog.'" Chaney laughed.

As the romantic lyrics played, she followed Drake's lead. He spun her around with ease. She loved to dance, but felt like a newbie compared to him. "How did you become such a good dancer?"

"My father. He never learned to dance, but thought I should." Drake shifted his hand to the small of her back. "He bartered car repairs for dance lessons."

"That's resourceful," Chaney said.

"He had to be."

Once again she heard the pride in his voice like the last time he'd talked about his dad. "I didn't know any boys who took dance lessons when I was growing up."

"Well, if any did, they most likely kept the fact to themselves." Drake pulled her closer. "I was teased by the other boys and even got into a fight or two over the dancing."

"A fight?" She liked talking about his past. That way she didn't have to think about how good dancing with him felt. "That's awful."

"Not so awful," he admitted. "I had the last laugh, because I learned how to sweep a girl off her feet."

Drake spun her around the dance floor again.

Dancing with him was almost magical. Shivery pulses of pleasure shot through her. "I bet you've only improved your techniques over the years."

"Perhaps, but I've never swept a queen off her feet." He gave her a smoldering stare. "Are you game?"

Her pulse quickened. She forced herself to breathe. It wasn't easy. "I don't play, remember?"

"There's always a first time," he said. "Remember you found your adventurous side at the castle."

She was tempted, but like then the line between reality and fantasy was blurring once again. She couldn't allow that to happen. Dancing would have to be enough. "I'm sure you could have your pick of any woman at the party, excluding Gemma, if you really wanted to sweep someone off her feet."

"I have the one I want right here."

"Guinevere, you mean."

Wicked mischief lit his eyes. "Of course, no one else but Guinevere will do tonight."

Chaney wanted to believe him. She wanted to…pretend and live the fantasy for just a while longer. "Then dance with your queen."

As they danced, her heels got tangled with the hem of her gown. His hands tightened around her.

She leaned so far forward, her chest bumped against Drake's armored breastplate.

"Sorry," she mumbled.

"I've got you."

That was what she was afraid of.

So much for fantasy. She'd just gotten doused with a bucketful of reality. Chaney straightened. She cleared her dry throat. "Thanks."

"The pleasure is all mine." His gaze remained fixed on her, as if no one else was dancing or in the crowded room with them. "My queen."

Her heart thumpity-thumped.

Chaney didn't know what to make of Drake Llewelyn. She wanted to pierce through the ever-so-charming, sinfully handsome exterior and learn more about the man inside, about his past, his hopes and his dreams.

"This is a first for me," he said, as if reading her mind.

"Dancing in armor."

"Yes, but I was thinking of having a song. I've never had a song with anyone I've dated."

"We're not dating," she said quickly. "Friends, remember."

"This feels like a date," he countered. "I picked you up. I'll take you home."

"Not home," she corrected. "Back to my hotel."

"I'll take you wherever you desire to go, my lady."

Right now she desired him. Chaney wet her lips. "I've never had a song with anyone, either."

"What about your fiancé?" Drake asked.

She thought for a moment. "No, we didn't have a song."

"Well, then this is a first for both of us."

Us.

The word reverberated through her.

With Drake's hands on her and hers on him, she felt like part of an us, one half of a couple, but the song about falling in love could never be their song. He would never play the fool by rushing into a relationship. And forget about him falling in love with her. That wasn't going to happen. He'd told her he wasn't looking for love, that he didn't want it.

But wearing this costume and playing his queen for the evening made his words easy to ignore. She couldn't do that. She squared her shoulders as if preparing for a battle, not finishing off a slow dance. "This song can be Lancelot's and Guinevere's. The lyrics fit them better than us."

Drake tipped his head. "Whatever you say, my queen."

The song ended, but his hands remained on her waist. Their gazes stayed locked on each other. A new song began. Something faster, louder.

Chaney realized she was still touching him and snatched her hands away. Something about him made her forget her manners and common courtesy. Not to mention common sense and her resolve to be immune to him. She was going to need a vaccination for that to happen, but the least she could do was separate herself from him now.

"I'm a bit warm in this gown," she said. "I think I'll wander out to the garden where it's cooler."

"I'll go with you," he offered.

So much for time away from him. She bit back a sigh, trying to focus on the good things he'd done, like putting on this party. He wasn't trying to make her feel all fluttery inside. At least, she hoped he wasn't.

Chaney wove her way through until she could step out the back door. The sudden drop temperature brought goose bumps to her arms, but the fresh air filled her lungs and cleared her mind.

"Cooler now?" Drake asked.

She nodded, but having him with her made her muscles tense. At least they didn't have to shout. The music and noise from inside was muted out here. "Your armor must be hot."

He raised a brow. "Just my armor?"

"I didn't know knights fished for compliments."

Drake laughed. "Knights fish for many things, but are not always successful in catching them."

Desire filled his dark eyes, make her feel as if she might be the next thing he wanted to hook and reel in. Better not go there. She took a deep breath. "Thanks for throwing this party for Gemma and making it possible for me to be here."

"That's what friends are for."

Friends. Thinking of him as only her friend would kill the fantasy growing in her head, a fantasy fueled by dancing together.

He walked toward her, an imposing figure, a tall, dark knight in armor and a beard. "I'm enjoying tonight."

"Me, too."

He ran the edge of his finger along her jawline. His touch sent tingles skittering through her.

"I know something that would make tonight even more enjoyable," he said softly.

"What?" she asked, sounding as breathless as she felt.

A devilish heat flared his eyes. "A kiss."

CHAPTER SIX

CHANEY'S heart slammed against her chest. "Bad idea."

"Seems like a damn good one to me."

"Not as long as I'm working for you."

Drake arched a brow. "I'm not your boss."

"Semantics." She struggled to hold on to a firm grasp of reality. But his finger, callused not smooth, lightly rubbing her face felt so good. "You own the cable channel. You're the executive producer of the show."

"You don't report to me."

He closed the space between them until his face was mere inches from hers. Chaney's heart felt as if it might explode from pounding so fast. "But—"

"You're leaving tomorrow."

She was. "I'm on the payroll until then."

"A kiss," he said. "Think about it."

Heaven help her, but she was thinking about

it. Just the thought heated the blood pulsing through her veins.

"What harm could come from one little kiss?" he asked.

Oh, she so wanted to believe him. But practicality pushed its way through his hypnotic charm. "Think Helen of Troy and Paris, Guinevere and Lancelot, Tristan and Isolde, Romeo and Juliet."

"That's a no then," Drake said.

Chaney said nothing. She couldn't. A part of her wanted to run far, far away. But another part wanted to kiss him so she'd know, know that what she'd walked away from four years ago wasn't worth dwelling on, know he wasn't really anything special now.

"Chaney…"

The affection in his voice made it difficult for her to remain immune from his charm. From him. She didn't want to give in to temptation even though she was flying home tomorrow and wouldn't be seeing him again. She was too afraid of being hurt.

Still her gaze kept returning to his lips. Lips she'd memorized years ago and dreamed about even now.

"If Guinevere were here, she would allow Lancelot to kiss her." Drake cupped Chaney's face lightly. "You agreed to be Guinevere tonight."

The desire in his eyes both thrilled and frightened her. Her resolve weakened. She didn't want to give up so easily. "For a noble knight, you're not playing fair."

His warm breath fanned her cheek. "One kiss is more than fair, my queen."

Anticipation shot from her lips all the way down to her toes. She swallowed. "Just one kiss?"

"Only one." He lowered his hand. "A goodbye kiss."

Slowly, as if giving her the chance to say no or back away again, he brought his mouth toward hers.

Every nerve ending tingled in hope. But a voice—common sense, perhaps?—shouted a warning.

Too late. She raised her chin and closed her eyes.

His lips touched gently against hers, as if joining something delicate or fragile.

Light, soft, tender.

His mustache and beard brushed her skin. She was surprised how soft the hair was. Not quite a ticklish feather, but not a scratchy whisker, either.

He kept his lips on hers, gentle yet firm.

The way he kissed made her feel cherished and adored, and she liked thinking he cared for her in that way. An inviting warmth, like a sunny day after a rainstorm, settled over her, making her feel as if she'd finally reached the destination she'd been seeking.

Drake kept his hands at his sides and only

touched her with his lips. Yet she felt a closeness, as if she were being embraced.

The taste of him filled her mouth. She soaked up the flavors—salt, wine, a hint of chocolate.

Not at all how she thought Drake Llewelyn would kiss, but it was enough to tell her what she'd known in her heart, what she'd feared.

One kiss would never be enough.

He brushed his hand through her hair, the strands sifting through his fingers. She leaned into the kiss. Into him.

She touched his face, feeling the smoothness of his cheek, the texture of his beard beneath her palm.

Her touch seemed to be the invitation he needed. His hands circled her waist and pulled her closer. She went eagerly, almost impatiently, toward him, placing her hands over the armor encasing his shoulders.

He increased the pressure against her mouth. She did the same, rising on tiptoe to get as close to him as the armor would allow. She wove her fingers through his wavy hair.

The gentleness of his kiss changed, slowly at first, then suddenly spiraling into something more. Something hot.

Sparks flared. Fire ignited. Passion grew.

Hunger took over. Chaney couldn't get enough of him, of his kisses. More, she wanted more.

Kiss after kiss filled her with pleasure. She shivered with wanting. Chaney took what he offered and gave back even more.

An ache grew deep within her. An ache only he could soothe.

As his lips moved expertly over hers, his tongue explored her mouth. Sensation crashed through her. Her knees went weak, and she clung to his armor to keep from sliding to the ground. His strong hands splayed against her back, drawing her closer. She longed to touch him, to feel the warmth of his skin, not the cool metal of his armor.

"Oh, Drake," she murmured.

He dragged his lips from hers and stepped back. His ragged breathing matched her own. Surprise filled his dark eyes.

Chaney stood with her hands at her side. She struggled to clear her head so she could think, but she was still awash in sensation. Her brain felt as if all gray matter had been replaced with cotton candy.

But she didn't mind.

She smiled, in awe of the man standing in front of her, the man who had kissed her as if his life depended on that one kiss.

On her.

Her lips throbbed. She fought the urge to touch them to see if they were as swollen and bruised as they felt. Instead she raised her hand to caress his face, to feel his warmth, to touch the soft hair on his face, to soak up his strength.

He inhaled deeply.

She lowered her arm to her side.

She'd never been kissed like that before. She couldn't imagine ever meeting someone else who could kiss her that way again. His kisses had stolen her breath and nearly captured her heart. A few more minutes, even seconds, and she would have surrendered. Gladly.

She could understand why Guinevere might have fallen for Lancelot if his kiss had made her feel half as special as Drake's kiss had made Chaney feel. All she wanted was to kiss him again.

Maybe one kiss wouldn't be enough for Drake, either.

Her smile widened. She sure hoped he felt that way. A long-distance relationship might not be entirely impossible. She would be willing to give it a try.

He stared at her with his dark eyes framed by ridiculously long eyelashes. No man had a right to be so gorgeous. Not that she was complaining. Especially if he kissed her again.

"You were right," he said.

She wet her lips. "About what?"

A muscle flicked at his jaw. "A kiss wasn't a very good idea at all."

* * *

What had he done?

When Drake had finished kissing Chaney, she'd stared up at him with such a look of wonder and hope in her hazel-green eyes, he couldn't breathe. The way she had touched his face so lovingly squeezed his heart like a vise. The flash of hurt and confusion in those same eyes now knifed him in the gut.

He dragged his hand through his hair. "I'm sorry, Chaney."

"Sorry?" She pursed her swollen, thoroughly kissed lips. "You're sorry you kissed me?"

Hell, yes. He had kissed other beautiful women with similar passion, but none had kissed him back making him feel as if she were the air he needed to breathe. She'd wanted more. Him, too.

Kissing Chaney had been like finding a hidden treasure, one he wanted to keep all to himself. Only the sound of her voice, a sexy murmur of his name, made Drake realize how close he was to losing control. Everything he thought he understood, everything he thought he knew had been flipped upside down and inside out.

With only one kiss.

His plan to get her out of his system had backfired. And now he needed her out of his life more than ever.

"Yes," Drake said.

"I see." Chaney pressed her lips together.

And so did he.

She had every right to be upset with him. He'd pursued her all evening, and the incredible kiss gave her the right to expect more. But it was the more that concerned him.

Okay, had him quaking in his boots.

She was so much more than a pair of soft lips, so much more than a pair of soft breasts pressed against him. She was so much more than he expected, so much more than he wanted.

Drake couldn't wait for her to go back home where she belonged. And he wasn't talking about the hotel. If he could, he'd send her back across the pond tonight.

Kissing her had sent his world spinning off its axis. He wanted his world back where it should be, thank you very much.

Chaney straightened. "Why did you kiss me?"

"I wanted to know…"

"Know what?"

"Know what kissing you would finally feel like." And now Drake wished he could turn back the clocks so he didn't. Forget about getting over her. He had a feeling her kiss would linger with him a long time.

So would her memory.

At least she would be far away from him.

Her steady gaze met his. "Yet you're sorry."

"I was selfish." And stupid. Drake had gone into the kiss thinking only about what he wanted—a kiss get her out of his mind once and for all, a goodbye. He hadn't acknowledged the consequences. That he might want more kisses, more of Chaney. His reaction was totally outside his comfort zone. Totally outside his experience or control.

That made her dangerous.

As Chaney kissed him back, he felt her seeping inside of him and heading straight to his heart. That place was off-limits. "You're leaving town tomorrow. I don't want you to think— It's not like we'll see each other again."

An excuse, Drake realized the moment the words left his mouth. He couldn't tell her the truth.

He had always been good at compartmentalizing things—his work, his father, the women he dated. But Chaney opened up all the doors and mixed things up. What belonged outside suddenly was inside. He didn't like that.

Worse, he'd lost himself while kissing her. Nothing but Chaney had mattered. He knew making a woman the entire focus of his world would be a huge mistake. He'd learned his lesson from his father. Love faded, leaving broken hearts and promises and loneliness. Drake wanted no part of that. "If I overstepped my—"

"It was one kiss," she interrupted. "And I kissed you back. No big deal. A goodbye kiss, right?"

Her words bristled like the quills of a porcupine. *No big deal.*

Maybe, or maybe not.

He hadn't mistaken her reactions or hunger during the kiss. He'd tasted her passion. Even her cheeks remained flushed.

Yet self-preservation kept his ego in check. And goodbye felt like a double-edged sword at the moment.

"What did you expect I would do?" she continued. "Beg you to take me to bed in spite of you thinking the kiss was a mistake? Or sue you for sexual harassment?"

Drake tried to imagine her doing either. He couldn't. "I didn't expect anything, actually. I just wanted to…"

"Remove any doubt."

"Yes."

"You've done that," she said. "No worries. I know where things stand."

"Friends."

"Oh, I don't think so." A car alarmed blared, then stopped. She looked toward the house, then her gaze returned pointedly to him. "Like you said, after tonight, we won't be seeing each other again."

Drake swallowed around the unexpected lump of panic, even though this was what he wanted—Chaney out of his life. "So, if we're not friends, what are we?"

"Co-workers." And then, so he couldn't possibly miss her hurt or her point, she added, "Former co-workers."

He winced. "I can live with that."

He would have to now.

Drake might be able to live with that, but could Chaney? She hadn't expected him to accept and go along with her suggestion to be former co-workers so easily. That hurt. And right now the only thing she wanted was for the ground to open up and swallow her whole.

She glanced around the garden, at the white birdbath near a tree, at a silly-looking gnome figure under a bush, at anything that wasn't Drake.

Chaney didn't know how long she stood there saying nothing. Not that it mattered. She already felt like a total fool, turning his kissing her into something big enough to want more, to want to take a chance on a relationship.

On love.

With him.

Pathetic.

She'd been so close to blurting out her thoughts

and feelings. She'd even thought of a long-distance relationship.

Chaney grimaced.

And then he called the entire episode a mistake, a mistake as if he'd gotten off at the wrong Tube stop or ordered the wrong size of coffee.

Stupid, stupid, stupid.

She needed to have her head examined. Still this was a lesson she needed to learn. Again. Not dating, good; kissing men like Drake, bad. Maybe one day she'd meet a nice, normal guy and want to date. But not now.

This proved she wasn't ready.

Goose bumps prickled her skin. She crossed her arms over her chest.

"You're cold," Drake said finally.

She forced herself not to turn and look at him. "I came out here to cool down."

"Cool is one thing. You're almost shivering."

She wished he hadn't noticed or sounded as if he cared. "I'm thinking of heading inside to see if Gemma needs anything."

"Good idea."

She hurried to the back door and into the house. The warmer temperature inside did nothing to drive the deep chill away. She still felt the urge to wrap her arms around herself. She was surrounded by people, but felt so alone.

The same way she felt when she was with her family. And like those times, she knew exactly what to do. Chaney pasted on a smile and squeezed past all the partygoers to make her way into the living room.

The volume of the music had increased, as had the noise level of conversations. She noticed the three women from earlier eyeing her. Then they disappeared. No doubt in search of their prey. They would probably be only too happy to be "friends" with Drake. Bitterness coated her mouth.

Well, they could have him. He wasn't her…problem. He wasn't her anything.

She headed toward the couch where Gemma lay.

The sight of Oliver whispering into his wife's ear stopped Chaney in her tracks. The couple looked at each other with a combination of affection and respect. Talk about hitting the romance jackpot. The two had found their perfect match. Unfortunately, she had never had that kind of luck.

Chaney touched her lips. At this rate she probably never would.

She eyed the dessert buffet, but thought better of eating more sweets. Instead she waited for Oliver to walk away and, once he had, knelt next to Gemma.

"Do you need anything?" Chaney asked.

"I have everything I need right here." Her friend's smile widened. "Where have you been?"

"The garden," Chaney admitted. "This costume is lovely, but it's also very warm."

"Are you sure dancing with Drake didn't heat you up?" Gemma teased, the way she had when they'd worked and lived together. That had been before Oliver, before Tyler, before so many things. "You were so right about him looking hot in that armor. He's practically scorching. The ratings are going to soar when that episode airs."

Thank goodness for the low lighting, Chaney thought. Her cheeks were red as she remembered what she'd told Gemma about the taping at the castle. "He makes a dashing knight."

"He's a good dancer, too."

"I only danced with him to save him from the circling sharks."

"I saw the hungry trio," Gemma said. "They didn't like how cozy the two of you looked."

"It was just a dance."

"Nothing more?" Gemma sounded curious.

Chaney thought about the kiss in the garden, about the way her lips still throbbed, about what he'd said to her afterward. "No, nothing."

Drake entered the living room. His gaze met and held hers for a moment. He looked away as the trio of women closed in on him.

A heave weight pressed down on Chaney. She forced a smile. "See, nothing."

"I do see," Gemma said. "And I'm relieved. You're one of my best friends, and Drake's the best boss in the world. But he's also a heartbreaker and a bad risk when it comes to relationships. I don't want to see you hurt again."

Too late.

Chaney had already been hurt. Okay, more embarrassed than hurt when he'd dashed her hopes by saying the kiss had been a mistake. And just now when she saw him with the three women, breathing had gotten a little harder.

Those things only reaffirmed she was doing the right thing.

If she felt like this after one kiss, what could Drake do to her if things got serious?

"Trust me, I don't want that to happen, either," Chaney said. "After tonight I'll probably never see Drake again."

Even if her selfish lips and her stupid heart might want her to.

On the way back to her hotel two hours later, Chaney sat alone in the back of the limousine, disappointed with Drake and with herself.

He had made a play for her, kissed her silly, made her believe in love and think long-distance relationship, before dropping her to hang with the Bimbo Trio for the rest of the evening.

Shame on him.

And shame on her.

Chaney stretched out her legs. The limousine seemed larger without Drake, who had stayed at the party and supervise cleanup so Oliver wouldn't have to worry about it. Better that Drake was there than here.

Yet she couldn't stop thinking about him, about the party. She had bumped into him on the dance floor, the moment awkward and tense. His hand kept her upright, and her body had immediately reacted to his touch.

Physical attraction. Chemistry. Just like his kisses. That was all it was. All it could ever be.

Chaney sighed.

She wanted to believe in happily ever after, that a man could love her the way she wanted to be loved, for who she was, nothing else. Drake had proven once again he wasn't that guy.

Well, I don't want Belle's love or anyone else's, so I don't have to worry about doing anything.

His words at the castle should have warned her away from him. She leaned her head back against the leather seat.

Her cell phone rang. Drake? She hated the way her heart leaped at the thought. She pulled it out of the purse and checked the number. Not Drake, her boss at the studio. It would be afternoon in Los Angeles now.

"Hello, Justin," she said. "What's going on?"

"I have some bad news, Chaney."

Oh, no. Her heart sank even lower. "I didn't get the promotion."

"No, you didn't, but it's more than that." He sighed. "The studio is cutting the budget by twenty-five percent and requiring head count reductions. While you've been away, we've been able to split your workload, so your position has been eliminated."

She listened in disbelief, trying to process what she'd been told. She'd been dumped. Again.

Dumped by Drake and now by her boss. All she needed was Tyler or Simone to call her, and Chaney would have a trifecta.

She took a deep breath and cleared her dry throat. "I completed the majority of my workload before I left, so my leave of absence wouldn't overwhelm any of you."

"It's a done deal, Chaney."

She didn't hear any regret in Justin's voice. Why not?

Wasn't she a good employee?

Tears stung her eyes. "So, just like that I'm fired?"

"Not fired," he corrected. "Laid off. On Monday you need to return your keys and ID. HR will explain your severance package, return your personal items from your cubicle and perform an exit interview with you."

Four years of hard work and loyalty and this was what it came down to, a late-night call taking away the one thing that had been going right in her life—her job.

She swallowed around the lump of emotion in her throat.

"If you have anything at home," Justin continued. "I trust you to turn it in."

Trust. Chaney nearly laughed. She'd trusted Justin when he said the leave of absence was no problem and she'd probably end up with a promotion when she returned. She'd also trusted Drake tonight when she'd kissed him back.

"Tell me one thing, please." She struggled to understand the logic behind the decision. She'd always had good reviews and been held up as a model employee. She'd never been disciplined or even warned about work or behavior. Even Drake and the people she'd worked with on the three episodes had all praised her. This made no sense. "Did I ever have a real shot at the promotion?"

Her boss, whom she'd work countless hours for to make him look good, didn't say a word. The silence on the line intensified, made her more uncomfortable. The same way she'd felt with Drake after he told her the kiss had been a mistake.

"Justin?" she asked.

"HR will respond to any questions you have on Monday morning," he said. "Good luck in the future, Chaney."

He hung up.

No "Thank you." No "Let's get everyone together for a goodbye drink." No answers.

Tonight proved what she should have known before. She was a lousy judge of character. She picked the wrong job, the wrong men and the wrong loyalties.

Chaney stared at the cell phone in her hand. What was she going to do?

"Enjoy your flight," the customer service representative at the gate said the next morning at Heathrow airport.

Chaney adjusted the prescription sunglasses hiding her puffy red and tired eyes. She'd tried to drown her emotions with ice cream last night. It hadn't helped. "Thank you."

Leaving London saddened her. Being laid off from her job stung. And losing Drake…

She sucked in a breath. Well, he was never hers to begin with. And the sooner she accepted that, the sooner she would stop feeling as if she had lost her best friend.

Chaney boarded the flight and found her seat. Thank goodness she had a window seat. All she wanted to do was buckle her seat belt and sleep for the next eleven hours or so.

But each time she closed her eyes, she thought about Drake or the phone call from Justin or Drake again. The same as it had been last night. And like then, she stopped trying to sleep and watched the inflight movie instead.

Just her luck…a romantic comedy with an impossibly perky heroine who never gave up and an improbably happy ending complete with the couple riding off into the sunset.

Yeah, right.

As the credits rolled, she closed her eyes, but once again thoughts of Drake filled her mind.

She remembered seeing him for the first time in the great hall at Abbotsford Castle. He'd had a sexy beard and the knight's costume on. She recalled the time they'd sat in the library talking, munching on cookies and drinking milk. She couldn't forget when he'd come to say goodbye to her with his rain-soaked hair curled into ringlets. Or kissing him in the garden.

Chaney squeezed her eyes shut, trying to stop the scenes from replying in her mind. It didn't help. At least she wouldn't have to keep seeing Drake the way she did with Tyler. And honestly, what had she and Drake shared except a few hours together and some amazing kisses?

Nothing really.

Once she was home, she would be too busy trying to find a job to think about him. The memories would fade.

A few hours later she stood in the baggage claim area at LAX. "What do you mean my luggage was lost?"

"Not lost," said a man wearing an airline's uniform. "Misdirected. Once your bags arrive, we'll have them delivered."

Just what she needed to top off a really bad twenty-four hours.

As Chaney walked outside to catch a shuttle van home, she turned on her cell phone. It beeped. A voice message. Chaney listened.

"Welcome home, sweetheart," her mother said. "Call me as soon as you can. I want to make sure you don't make any plans for tomorrow night. We're having a dinner party. Everyone wants to hear about your trip."

Her mom made it sound as if Chaney had been on vacation, not working her tail off and getting her heart bruised.

She grimaced.

Dealing with her family and their friends for an entire evening was so not what she needed to do right now.

Chaney glanced around at the passengers with suitcases and laptop cases.

What she needed was a knight in shining armor to whisk her away. An image of a bearded Drake popped into her mind.

Scratch that. What she really needed was…a new life.

Drake wanted to get his life back to normal.

Sitting in his limousine, he adjusted his tie. The gallery opening tonight was exactly the kind of even he had always enjoyed attending. Four of his favorite things would be there—art, food, wine, women.

One of the newer assistants on the seventeenth floor, a cheerful girl with short, spiked hair, had invited him to her sister's first show. Drake was more than happy to say yes to the invitation. A brief appearance by him at a new artist's show would create buzz and bring much needed publicity. It was the least he could do for his employee and her sister.

Except…

Making others happy usually made him feel good himself, but tonight didn't feel as satisfying as it should. Not the way surprising Gemma last night had made him feel. Maybe once he arrived at the gallery, he would get that feeling back.

"How much further, Edward?" Drake asked.

"We're almost there, sir." His longtime chauffeur yawned.

No doubt Edward was tired from working late last night. "I appreciate you putting in the long hours yesterday. Feel free to go home after you drop me off at the gallery."

"Thank you, sir, the missus will appreciate my coming home early, but last night wasn't so bad. Easier for me than Miss Sullivan."

Chaney. Drake straightened. "In what way?"

"Well, that call from her boss."

"What call?"

Edward glanced in the rearview mirror. "If she didn't say…it's not really my place…"

"If I know what happened, I can help her."

"Yes, sir." Edward signaled to change lanes. "She received a call on the way back to the hotel. Let go, she was."

Bloody hell. Drake leaned forward. "Fired?"

Edward nodded in the rearview mirror. "Took me a minute to figure it out myself. Very professional, she was. I asked if she needed anything. She wanted ice cream, so I stopped at a market before dropping her off at her hotel."

"Thank you." Drake should have been the one helping her. He was used to taking care of everyone and fixing things. Yet Chaney hadn't called him and when she'd needed help.

She hadn't even told him she got fired.

That annoyed and upset him.

Chaney was the one person he wanted to take care of, the one person who'd gone out of her way to help him by taking a temporary leave of absence from her job. If she was paying the ultimate price—unemployment—for that help, Drake needed to do something about that.

He brushed his hand through his hair.

She should have called him.

Except…

There was no way she would have called, not after what happened in the garden. Guilt lodged in his throat. Things had gotten too personal between them. This just proved mixing work with personal matters was a bad idea.

But Drake wasn't going to let Chaney's not calling him stop him. He needed to find her and fix this.

This wasn't personal. This was what good bosses did. What he was going to do.

Whether she wanted his help or not.

CHAPTER SEVEN

ON SUNDAY afternoon, Chaney sat on her couch with her robe wrapped around her and slippers on her feet. She held a pint of Ben & Jerry's New York superfudge-chunk ice cream in one hand and a spoon with the other.

"Hi, Mom, Dad, everyone I've known my entire life." She practiced what she would say at her parents' dinner party tonight. "No, I didn't bring a date, but since so many of you are afraid I've stopped liking men, you'll be happy to know I've got a crush on this billionaire playboy who thinks kissing me was a huge mistake."

She ate a spoonful of ice cream.

"Oh, yeah, and you know that promotion I was going after at the studio? Didn't get it. Instead I lost my job. That's right, I'm unemployed."

She stabbed the spoon into the container and scooped another bite.

"And before I forget, I'm sorry for wearing

sweatpants tonight, but the airlines lost my luggage. Not that any of my pants would fit after I've eaten nothing but ice cream for the past two days."

Staring into the half-empty pint, she grimaced.

"This is *so* not going to go well tonight. The total failure of the daughter voted Girl Most Likely To Succeed by her high school senior class. Simone will think it's Christmas."

The doorbell rang.

Chaney stood.

Her luggage must have arrived from wherever it had been misdirected.

With her pint of ice cream in hand, she padded her way to the front door and opened it.

Drake.

The air whooshed from her lungs. She opened her mouth to speak, but her tongue felt too thick and no words would come out.

"Hello there, Chaney."

His accented voice disarmed her. The way he looked in his dark jacket, a striped button-down shirt and black jeans made her weak in the knees. The container of ice cream slipped from her hand.

He caught the pint in midair and handed it to her. "I'm a Cherry Garcia fan myself."

Chaney blinked in case she was dreaming again. When she opened her eyes, he was still standing there. She touched her unwashed hair and glanced down at the furry robe she was wearing. She must look frightful. "What are you doing here?"

"I happened to be in the neighborhood…"

She gave him a don't-mess-with-me look.

Concern filled his brown eyes. "How are you?"

Chaney didn't want his pity. She pulled her robe tighter. "Fine."

"Sick?"

"No." She should have said yes. She was in her bathrobe in the middle of the day. But the ice cream was probably a dead giveaway that she wasn't sick.

"My driver told me about you being laid off," Drake admitted. "I feel responsible. If you hadn't taken that leave of absence to help me out, things might have turned out differently for you."

"Thanks for your concern, but none of this is your fault. I wanted to take the leave of absence to work on the show so I could get more production experience. No regrets about that."

What she regretted was kissing him. She'd gotten caught up in the whole Lancelot fantasy. She wouldn't allow herself to believe it could be anything more.

And that's when she realized…he no longer looked like a knight.

"Your beard is gone."

He ran his hand over his smooth face. "Halloween has passed. I've put the armor away, too."

If only she could tuck her attraction away so easily.

She thought once he'd shaved his beard, erasing the whole knight archetype and fantasy that had been brewing in her dreams these past couple of weeks, she'd feel different about him. That her attraction would disappear. And so would her desire to kiss him again.

But she didn't, it hadn't, and she still did.

"I have a proposal for you."

Her heart lodged in her throat. Proposal, as in marriage proposal? Okay, she realized after about a nanosecond, that was a really stupid thing to think. "I'm listening."

"Come work for me."

"What?"

"Be the show's associate producer during the final taping," he explained. "Once the episode's completed, you can continue with *The Billionaire's Playground* while Gem's on maternity leave or find a different position at the Dragon Channel or do something completely different within Dragon Llewelyn."

"You're offering me a job, just like that?"

"We discussed my reasons for wanting to hire you at the castle."

Chaney thought about the surprise party. The mix of emotions and memories clouded her brain. "That was before you kissed me."

His lips thinned. "The kiss was no big deal, remember?"

"I remember." No big deal compared to a 7.0 earthquake. She'd been trying to protect herself when she'd said those words and with good reason. He'd called the kiss a mistake, when she'd felt it was the most perfect thing in the world. "I just want to make sure everything is out in the open and clear."

"That's usually my line."

"I'm a fast learner."

"I like that about you," Drake pulled out a plane ticket from his jacket pocket and handed it to her. "Here."

She opened the folder. A round-trip ticket from LAX to NAS. Los Angeles to Nassau. "A plane ticket with my name on it."

"Yes."

She read the date. "Leaving tomorrow."

"Yes."

"You just made me the offer. I haven't said yes."

"Say yes, then," he urged. "There's nothing stopping you."

Oh, yes, there was. She was stopping herself. "I won't be rushed into this."

Against her better judgment like she'd been rushed into that kiss, that…mistake. Wariness enveloped her.

"I don't want to rush you, but the taping this week," he said. "If you want to work on the episode, you must leave tomorrow."

Chaney could understand that, but still… She didn't know if she could trust him, if she could trust herself. She'd misjudged people so badly before. She couldn't do it again. "This is a great opportunity, but I need to think it over."

"Take all the time you need. I want you in the Bahamas, but if you're not ready, you can forget about the taping and decide if you're interested in the rest of my offer," he said. "I'd be a fool to lose someone so hardworking and talented to another company."

For once Chaney felt as though she held the higher ground with him. It was a good feeling. "What does Gemma think about this?"

Chaney hadn't told Gemma about losing her job because she didn't want her friend to worry.

"Gem doesn't know I'm here or about you being laid off. As far as she's concerned, there isn't going to be an associate producer at the taping."

Drake was protecting Gemma, too. Chaney appreciated his chivalrous behavior, but a question remained. "Is this job offer really about making sure Gemma doesn't feel responsible for my being laid off?"

His gaze collided with Chaney's. "Not at all."

A connection that had nothing to do with friendship or working together drew her toward him. She forced her feet to remain where they were, on the tiled entryway of her apartment.

"You'll be an asset to the crew, the channel and Dragon Llewelyn," he continued. "I don't have a lot of deadwood or extra layers of management costing me money. I expect hard work, but you will be rewarded for the hours you put in. Your job will be secure."

Chaney wanted to believe him. She needed a job, and she loved working on the show and with the crew. But spending more time with Drake would only intensify her attraction for him. An attraction that would go nowhere, she reminded herself. Not only because he would be her boss, but also because they had totally opposite views of love. "What if we set a trial period? You can see if my performance is up to par."

"I don't need a trial period."

"I do."

A muscle pulsed at his jaw. "Fine, you can have a trial period. Say the end of the taping."

Yes. She felt the urge to pump her fist but didn't. "I may need longer."

"You set the timetable and tell me when you're ready to discuss staying on permanently."

A man walked to the door of her apartment with her suitcase and garment bag. "Chaney Sullivan?"

"Yes."

"Here are your bags." He set them next to Drake. "Sign here, please."

By the time she handed back the man's pen and thanked him, Drake had carried the luggage inside.

He stood in her living room. "Nice place."

"Thanks." Chaney felt rude for not inviting him in before, but he'd caught her off guard. He had a bad habit of doing that. She stepped inside and closed the door.

He motioned to the empty pint of ice cream setting on the coffee table. "Death by chocolate?"

"Not a bad way to go. Especially if it would keep me from having to go out tonight." Chaney ate a spoonful of the ice cream in her hand. "Would you like some? I have another pint in the freezer."

"No, thanks." His assessing gaze washed over her, making Chaney feel half a step above a bag lady. "I like your bunny slippers."

She wiggled her toes so the floppy ears moved. "The slippers were a Christmas present from my Aunt Naomi."

"And the fuzzy lime-green robe?" he asked.

"A birthday present for myself."

"Interesting."

"Not really." Chaney glanced down at what she was wearing. "I love the color green, the fabric is soft and the fit quite comfortable."

He laughed. "You're the only person I know who could make such an impractical-looking robe seem practical."

She frowned. "My practicality is one of my assets. It's what led me to accept the job on a trial basis to make sure it's a good fit for me and you, I mean, Dragon Llewelyn.

He tipped his head. "I apologize to your practicality."

A beat passed and another. The atmosphere wasn't uncomfortable, but the underlying tension felt strange.

"Would you like to sit down?" she asked, not knowing what else to say.

"Thanks." Drake sat. "I hope I'm not keeping you from anything. You mentioned going out, or rather not wanting to go out tonight."

"My parents are having some family and friends over for dinner, and I'm invited. I tried begging off due to jet leg and a rotten mood, but no go. So I will spend the evening listening to comments about all my failures, starting with my dating status or lack of a date." She realized she was rambling, but couldn't stop herself. "Of course, I'm sure my being laid off will be added to the mix if anyone has talked to my parents."

She'd told them the news in a phone call yesterday. Their sympathy had made Chaney run out and buy more ice cream.

"Don't forget, you were only unemployed for a short time," Drake said. "You can now tell them that you are gainfully employed at the Dragon Channel or Dragon Llewelyn. Take your pick."

"That's right." She brightened. "Thanks to you."

He smiled.

She felt a hitch in her breath. "I'd better put the ice cream away and try to make myself presentable for the dinner."

"Let me help."

Chaney stiffened. "Get ready?"

He laughed. "I'm better at messing up hair than fixing it."

At least he was honest. "Then what are you talking about?"

"I'd be happy to accompany you as your date tonight, if that would make things go smoother for you."

Her gaze flew to his. "You would do that?"

He nodded. "I try to help my employees out if I can."

And she was his employee now.

At least on a trial basis.

Bringing him along would make things easier, except…

"It's generous of you to offer, but if you came along, people might assume we were—"

"Dating," he finished for her.

"Yes, and since you're my new boss…"

"I'm not your boss until tomorrow." The gold flecks in his eyes seemed brighter. "Let them think what they want tonight. We know the truth. That's all that matters."

She listed the pros and the cones. The pros were winning, but—

"We can take my limo."

"Yes." She normally avoided playing the one-up game with Simone, but this time Chaney was willing to take her turn. "I think I'm going to like the perks that come with working for you."

"Just wait." His charming grin curled her toes. "You haven't seen anything yet."

Drake sat next to Chaney in the limousine while they rode toward a suburb of Los Angeles. He'd gotten more than he bargained for tonight—an associate producer for the final episode, and longer if all went well with the "trial period," as well as a date.

But he was here to make amends.

For her losing her job and for…other reasons.

He glanced her way. She looked beautiful in a brown skirt, lace-trimmed shirt, fitted jacket and boots. Not that he minded what she'd had on before she changed.

The sight of Chaney in the Muppet-creature robe of hers with sad, vulnerable eyes and a smudge of chocolate ice cream on the corner of her mouth had almost made him take her in his arms and kiss her until she smiled. *Almost* being the operative word.

She'd appealed to him on a different level today. He'd found her defensiveness adorable, not annoying. She showed him she wasn't so perfect and competent, with everything in her life all neat and tidy all the time.

That Chaney he could handle. He could help her out the same way he did others. She would get what she needed, and he would get a grateful, loyal employee. Another win-win situation. His favorite kind.

"We're almost there." She sounded a little nervous.

The limousine turned onto a side street. Drake stared out the window at the large homes, big front yards and tree-lined sidewalks. Expensive SUVs and sports cars filled the driveways.

"This is where I grew up," she said.

He thought about the apartment over the garage

where he grew up. A far cry from this. Now he could afford to buy every house on the block, but owning a big, expensive house didn't make a house a home, and it was too late to bring his mother back, since she'd died twenty years ago.

"I'd like to raise my family in a neighborhood like this," she continued.

"You said you weren't interested in settling down."

"Not now, but someday."

"That's right," he said. "You're a romantic, one who believes in true love and prefers flowers to hearts and violins."

"It's good you remember those things if you're pretending to be my date."

"I am your date."

She looked at him with her brows drawn together. "Then if anyone asks, my favorite color is—"

"Green."

"How did you know?"

"You mentioned it." He thought about her robe again. "But no one is going to ask me your favorite color."

"I wouldn't put anything past Simone." Chaney pointed out a white Colonial-style two-story house. "That's my parents' house."

The limousine pulled to the curb in front of a cascading fountain with a nicely trimmed lawn surrounding it. The engine stopped. A minute later the chauffeur opened the door for them. Drake followed her out.

Chaney stood on the sidewalk, staring at her parents' house with a hint of panic in her eyes. She nibbled on her bottom lip. She looked scared, not vulnerable the way she had earlier this afternoon.

Drake wished she'd smile. He squeezed her hand. "You have a new job and a date. That's all anyone needs to know tonight."

She held on to his hand. For comfort or show, he didn't care. Even though he probably should. But tonight was for Chaney.

"I don't know how to thank you for coming with me," she said.

He could imagine a few ways, but knew those things would never happen given the circumstances. "You helped me by filling in for Gem. You agreed to a trial period when you could have just said no. Being here with you tonight is the least I can do."

The gratitude in her eyes tightened his throat. "Quid pro quo," she said.

Not exactly. Still he nodded.

"Well, we'd better get this over with."

He kept his fingers entwined with hers as they walked side by side up the brick pathway. He'd never been much of a hand holder, but he liked the feel of Chaney's hand in his.

They reached the front step.

"I guess this is it." Chaney parted her lips, an invitation almost a plea. One he couldn't ignore. Not when he was here to help her, to do whatever she needed him to do.

Drake brushed his lips over hers.

Sweet. She tasted like peppermint. He wanted another taste.

Chaney gave him one. She increased the pressure of her lips. He followed her lead by pulling her toward him. Her breasts pressed against him. This time no armor got in the way.

He liked this; he liked her.

The kiss intensified.

Drake trailed kisses along her jaw until he reached her ear. He nibbled on her lobe, getting her to arch even closer to him. Pleasure radiated outward.

Her mouth sought his with an eagerness that surprised him. Drake was happy to oblige and recaptured her lips with his.

He heard a noise. Footsteps. Maybe something else. He was too busy enjoying kissing Chaney to think about anything else.

"Chaney?" a feminine voice asked.

She jerked away from him so fast she nearly fell backward off the step. He tightened his hold on her.

The front door was now open. Drake recognized the two people standing with surprised expressions from the photograph he'd seen in Chaney's bedroom. Her mother was an attractive woman with brown hair and a wide smile. Her father was taller than he'd expected with white hair and a cautious expression on his face.

"M-Mom, D-Dad," Chaney stuttered. Her cheeks flushed. "Hi."

"Welcome home, sweetie." Her mother wiped her hands on her apron and hugged Chaney. "I thought I heard a car pull up out front. We were hoping it was you."

Her father's eyes left Drake's only long enough to check the limousine parked at the curb. "Hello."

"This is Drake Llewelyn." Chaney sounded breathless, but as soon as she said his name her father straightened. "These are my parents, Barbara and Patrick Sullivan."

Drake extended his arm. "It's nice to meet you, Mr.—"

"Patrick is fine." Her father's handshake was firm. "Nice of you to join us tonight."

Barbara nodded. "We're delighted to meet you, Drake."

"The pleasure is mine." He found it amusing Chaney's parents were die-hard horror movie fans. They looked more like bridge players or foodies. "Chaney talked about you when she was in London."

"Only good things, I hope," Patrick teased.

"Of course, honey." Barbara patted his arm. "It's Chaney. She's a good girl."

Drake wasn't about to differ. She was a good worker, friend and kisser. And not in that particular order.

"I should have called and let you know I was bringing a guest." The words spewed from Chaney's mouth like water over a crumbling dam. Her nerves seemed to be getting to her. "But—"

"I flew in unannounced this afternoon and surprised your daughter," Drake interrupted, to take some pressure of Chaney. "I hope my being here is not an inconvenience."

"None at all." Barbara's green eyes twinkled. He had no trouble imagining her baking cookies and cupcakes on a daily basis. Though with her thin build, he doubted she sampled any of her creations. He'd guess Patrick did all the taste tests around here. "Any…friend of Chaney's is more than welcome."

"Thank you," he said.

Patrick motioned them into the house. "Come inside and meet everyone."

Drake placed his hand at the small of Chaney's back. "After you, darling."

Her parents exchanged pleased-looking glances. Two down, the rest of the family to go.

Drake wasn't concerned. The chemistry between him and Chaney was pretty obvious to anyone who looked for it.

He followed her inside. The scent of basil and garlic filled the air. The interior of the house reminded Drake of a home magazine layout. Every piece, each accessory, coordinated. Nothing out of place, nothing mismatched. The decor and neutral palette reminded him of Chaney's apartment except for the horror movie posters hanging on every wall. "You have a lovely house."

"Thank you." Barbara's grin widened. "I love decorating. I did Chaney's apartment."

So that explained the similarities. After seeing the robe she'd bought for herself, he would have expected her place to have a bit more color.

"I hope you like Italian food," Barbara said to him.

He flashed her his most charming smile. "It's one of my favorites."

Barbara beamed. "I baked biscotti, too. Chocolate."

"Chaney must love those," Drake said.

"She does." Barbara's danced with excitement. The same way he'd seen Chaney's eyes look. "Which is why I made them."

They entered a large, crowded room connected to the kitchen.

"Chaney and Drake are here," Barbara announced.

She made them sound like a couple, which, he realized, was the point of all this.

As introductions were made, he tried to keep track of who was who. Many of the women looked alike with similar haircuts and color highlight. The men played the who-has-the-harder-handshake game. But all the while, Drake heard murmurings in the background.

"Is that who I think it is?"

"Let's hope she has better luck holding on to him."

"Isn't he that billionaire on TV?"

"It'll never last."

"Did you hear she was fired?"

"I bet Tyler's relieved he married Simone instead."

Who were these people? Drake stared at each one of them with their pasted-on smiles and drinks in hand. But Chaney was the one who really surprised him. Her smile never faltered. Of course, it wasn't a real one because the smile didn't reach her eyes or even bring out a hint of her dimple.

He didn't know how she put up with this. Her parents seemed nice but oblivious to what they were putting their daughter through with this dinner.

No wonder Chaney hadn't wanted to come tonight. No doubt she had heard the unkind whispers and mumbles before or she wouldn't be so adept at ignoring them. She needed to get away from this environment. He would see that she did.

Drake made the rounds with Chaney, learning names and making nice the way a good boyfriend would. He ended up near a table filled with appetizers—antipasto, vegetable crudité, bruschetta and mini pizzas—with a couple he hadn't met yet.

"Drake Llwelyn, I want you to meet my sister, Simone, and her husband, Tyler," Chaney said.

So these were the two who had broken Chaney's heart. Drake reminded himself to be civil. For her sake. "Hello."

"Nice to meet you." Simone gave a half smile and appeared unimpressed. She reminded him of the stereotypical American high school cheerleader—short, bubbly, busty. The type of girl boys dreamed about having sex when they were sixteen. She looked at Chaney with disdain. "We were wondering if you were going to show up."

"I told you she'd be here." Tyler picked up one of the pizzas. He had the kind of all-American jock look that women would find appealing, but his hair was already starting to thin on top. "Chaney never lets anybody down."

Unlike you, Drake thought. "It's my fault we're late. I surprised Chaney with a visit."

Simone smirked. "That's nice of you to offer a shoulder to cry on."

"What do you mean by that?" Chaney asked her sister.

"Mom told me about you losing your job," Simone said almost gleefully. "I'm sure that has to hurt, since work is pretty much your entire life."

Meow. Simone needed to put away her claws and grow up.

"The job was holding Chaney back." Drake placed his arm around her. He liked how she fit tucked against him. "It's worked out for the best."

"I agree." Chaney leaned into him. "It's definitely for the best."

"I'm Tyler Wincroft," the ex-turned-brother-in-law idiot said. "I enjoy your show."

"It's a nice hobby, and it brought Chaney and me back together so I have no complaints." Drake kissed the top of her head. "What do you do?"

"I work for Patrick. I'm a financial analyst."

"Nothing like a little job security working for your wife's father, eh?" Drake asked.

Chaney looked up at him with eyes full of laughter.

Tyler reached for another pizza. Simone flipped her hair behind her shoulder. Barbara and Patrick joined them. One big, happy family.

Drake was happy he only had his dad.

"So what brings you to Los Angeles, Drake?" Patrick asked.

"Chaney."

Barbara added another platter of bruschetta to the table. "Will this be a short visit?"

"Yes, since Chaney's flying out tomorrow."

"You just got home." Simone's panicked gaze darted between her sister and Drake. "Where are you going now?"

Drake set his jaw. "Chaney is…"

She placed her hand on his arm.

He gave a slight nod.

"I'm flying to the Bahamas after I pay a visit to the studio to drop off a few things and pick up my severance pay."

The noise in the room dropped down to a few whispers. Others at the party seemed to be listening closely to the conversation. Drake wasn't surprised since somehow Chaney had become everyone's punching bag. He had a feeling her sister had something to do with that.

"What are *you* going to do in the Bahamas?" Simone asked, sounding slightly shrill.

Chaney raised her chin. "Work as the associate producer on *The Billionaire's Playground.*"

Simone pouted. Tyler stared at the buffet table.

Barbara gave Chaney a hug. "That's wonderful news, sweetheart."

"How long will you be gone?" Patrick asked.

This was Drake's cue. He pulled Chaney to him, so her back was against his chest, and wrapped his arms around her. The position felt totally natural and comfortable, surprisingly so. "I'm hoping she'll be gone a very long time."

The words were true, too. He didn't want Chaney here. He wanted her with…him. For work, he rationalized.

The lines around Barbara's mouth deepened. "Why is that, Drake?"

"Because I'm trying to convince Chaney to leave Los Angeles and move to London."

Again, not a lie. She would thrive in London at the company headquarters. Plus Gemma was there. The two were close.

Tyler held a half-eaten carrot stick in his hand. "What's so great about London?"

Once again, Drake deferred to Chaney.

A warm smile, complete with her adorable dimple, brightened Chaney's entire face. "London is where Drake lives."

CHAPTER EIGHT

AFTER the dinner party, Chaney stood in front of her apartment door with Drake at her side. She wanted to invite him in. She wanted to kiss him.

To thank him.

He'd given her a job. He'd pretended to be her date. He'd saved her from appearing like a total failure in front of her family.

Quid pro quo. She owed him. Big-time. "Thanks! You went above and beyond at my parents' house, being such an awesome 'boyfriend.'"

"I was happy to do it." He spoke as if he'd merely held open a door for her, not saved her from a night of living hell.

"I really appreciate it. You, I mean. You made things so much easier."

"Easier, perhaps, but even if I hadn't been there, you wouldn't have been a failure."

"Oh, yes, I would have been." She looked down at the welcome mat. "It wouldn't have been pretty."

"Well, you were pretty tonight."

"Thank you."

"You know, they might be your family, but you don't have to define yourself by their terms and pretend just so you get along," he said. "You are perfect exactly the way you are."

His words wrapped around her heart like a big, cozy hug. She stared at him amazed, unsure, grateful. "No one's every said that to me before."

"It's true."

He sounded genuine. She bit her lip. "I want to believe you."

"Then do."

"You make it sound so simple."

"It is simple," he said. "No reason to complicate it."

A little late for not complicating things. Right now she wished he could be her real boyfriend. She sighed.

Chaney stared up at him. The warmth in his eyes blanketed her like a quilt. Wrapping herself up in him sounded pretty good. "I'll try."

"That's my girl," he said with that delicious accented voice of his. "Your family does care about you, even if they have a funny way of showing it. Your father pulled me aside for a little chat."

Drake had been at her side most of the time.

"Somehow I must have missed when that happened."

"You were in the kitchen with your mother."

"Oh." Chaney remembered. "That's when my mom wanted the lowdown on you."

"Your father wanted the same from me," Drake said. "He even poured me a brandy."

"No fair," Chaney teased. "I only got another biscotti."

He laughed. "I would have preferred a cookie."

"So what did my dad say?" she asked.

"He told me a change of scenery would do you good and said London seemed to agree with you. Then he asked me what my intentions were toward you."

"He didn't."

"He did."

"Oh, no. That must have totally awkward and…"

"Charmingly old-fashioned," Drake said softly. "I respect a man who cares so much about his daughter's welfare and happiness."

Curiosity got the best of her. "What did you tell him?"

"The truth."

"The truth that you weren't really my date."

"No," Drake said. "That I had only your best interests at heart and didn't want to see you get hurt."

Her heart melted. His words echoed what she

hoped a man would say if she were interested in pursuing a relationship with him. "You've really got this boyfriend—I mean—boss thing down."

He tucked a strand of hair behind her ear. The intimate gesture sent her heart pounding. "Tonight I wasn't being your boss."

She stared at up him with anticipation, hoping he wasn't ready to go back to being her boss just yet.

He ran the side of his fingertip along her cheek. "I liked being your date."

Chaney leaned toward him. Her lips longed for another kiss. "Me, too."

"And since this was a date, the night should end with one of these."

The feel of his lips moving over hers sent tingles of pleasure shooting through her.

If this wasn't real, she didn't care. It felt real. That was all she needed to know.

His touched caressed. His taste satiated.

She kissed him back. Not only with her lips but her heart.

Chaney didn't want to think about tomorrow or even five minutes from now. Only this moment, with his lips pressed against hers. Only this moment mattered.

As she relaxed against him, he slowly pulled away from her.

She looked up at him, wanting to understand,

seeking reassurance. What she found in his eyes was…regret.

Not again.

A heavy weight pressed down on the center of her chest.

"We can't forget," he said gently. "That I will be your boss again."

I always like to make sure and remove any doubt. It saves me from misunderstandings down the road as well as missed opportunities.

The line had been drawn. A much-needed line, if she admitted the truth to herself and her heart. She swallowed a sigh and attempted a smile.

It wasn't easy.

Disappointment mixed with relief. Chaney concentrated on the latter. Her heart didn't want to get hurt. She couldn't forget that no matter how good his kiss made her feel or how wonderful a future with him might seem.

She straightened. "And I'll be your associate producer."

Her gaze met his in understanding.

"Thanks for a wonderful evening, Chaney."

"Thank you for helping me out tonight."

The words sounded so formal, so wrong. Even though they stood inches away from each other, the distance between them seemed to grow, pushing them farther apart.

Chaney didn't know how to stop it. If she could or if she should.

A beat passed. Tension crackled in the air.

Drake started to speak, then stopped himself. "Don't forget to pack sunscreen."

He sounded like one of her parents. Or a…boss. "I won't."

"Good night, then," he said. "I'll see you in the Bahamas."

Chaney nodded, but apprehension gnawed at her.

You are perfect just the way you are.

He liked her as she was.

And he had hired her to be his associate producer.

Whatever she pretended to her family, she couldn't fool herself. Drake Llewelyn would never be more than her boss.

With sugar-white sand beneath his bare feet, Drake walked along the beach with his father, Rhys Llewelyn. The blue sky stretched all the way to the horizon, providing the perfect backdrop for a seagull's acrobatics. A breeze carried the scent of salt.

Home.

His little piece of heaven usually filled Drake with peace, but not today. He'd been preoccupied by one thing.

Chaney.

For the past two days she'd been on his mind, in his thoughts and haunting his dreams. He wanted only to see her, to remind himself that things had to remain professional if he wanted her to stay with Dragon Llewelyn.

Mixing business with pleasure had proved problematic with Chaney. She'd allowed their personal interactions—okay, kisses—to get in the way. That was what kept her from asking for his help when she'd gotten laid off. He wouldn't make the same mistake again.

His cat, Elliot, sprinted onto the beach. He must have followed them down from the house. The feline, a tortoiseshell tabby, loved playing on the fine sand.

Rhys breathed in deeply. "It's good to be home."

"A helluva lot warmer than London, that's for sure."

Drake noticed his dad took shorter steps and moved slower than he had during their holiday in Scotland. Maybe he should have brought his father back to the island sooner instead of letting him head off on another golf adventure alone. "You seem tired today, Dad."

"Jet lag and too many rounds of golf, that's all," Rhys said. "Not all of us have the energy you do."

"I'll call the doctor."

The cat pounced. Sand flew into the air.

"You'll do no such thing." Rhys brightened. The kick to his step returned. "Who is that breath-taking siren playing in the water?"

Drake looked from his cat to the shore, where Chaney waded through the turquoise water in a red-and-black one-piece swimsuit. His gaze zeroed in on her with the precision of a high-powered tele-scope. Every nerve ending stood at attention.

He stopped walking.

Damn, she was perfect just the way she was. He blew out a puff of air.

With her wet hair slicked back from her glowing face, she did look like a siren ready to lure a man to sea. Drake looked back at Elliot who pawed at the sand. "That's my new associate producer."

"Now I know why you were thinking about her instead of golf," Rhys said. "And why you like hosting the show so much."

Drake took another peek at Chaney as she jumped over a wave. Her breasts bounced. His mouth went dry. "I've never had an associate producer who looked that good in a swimsuit."

"Let's hope it's not the last time," Rhys said. "She's gorgeous."

"Don't let those long legs of hers fool you, Dad. She's as capable as she is…"

"Sexy," his father offered.

The adjective was spot-on. Drake had always

preferred bikinis, but he would have to rethink his opinion regarding the appeal of one-pieces now. Chaney's swimsuit clung to her, showing off her sensuous curves and pert breasts. He wouldn't mind peeling the fabric away to see her flat stomach and belly button. "She's an employee."

"Not my employee."

Mine.

Drake couldn't forget that if he wanted to help Chaney get her career back on track.

"There's nothing wrong with looking, son."

Except he wouldn't mind touching, too. And doing so would be…wrong on so many levels. Time to pull himself together. "Chaney isn't the type of woman who tries to flaunt her attractiveness so men look at her."

"Chaney. That name sounds familiar." His father looked up as if the answer was written in the sky. "She's the American. A former intern of yours."

Drake stared dumbfounded. "How…?"

"You mentioned her a few times. Though it's been some years now."

He didn't know why he would have mentioned Chaney to his dad. "It's been over five years since she was an intern."

"Looks like she's all grown-up."

No kidding. She waded to shore, looking like a vision or a partially clothed centerfold. The fullness of her breasts, the beading of her nipples and the curve from her narrow waist to her hips sent desire rocketing through Drake.

Elliot ran back to him and meowed. Needing a distraction, Drake picked up the tabby, pulled out a treat from his pocket and fed it to the cat. But his attention immediately returned to Chaney.

The waves lapped at her legs.

Her gaze connected with his for an instant before she looked away. She pressed her lips together and crossed her arms over her chest. Trying to cover herself, he wondered. The self-conscious act made her that much more appealing.

As she walked toward him, Drake felt a strange feeling grab hold in his stomach. He understood attraction, but this felt like something else. Something more. Something different. He'd missed her.

"You made it," she said, her gaze not quite meeting his.

"Yes."

A rivulet of water ran down her right leg. His groin tightened. He focused on her face.

"Excuse my son's sudden lack of manners." Rhys extended his arm to Chaney. "I'm Rhys Llewelyn. Drake's father."

"Chaney Sullivan." She shook hands and then picked up a colorful piece of fabric lying on a beach towel. "It's so nice to meet you."

"The pleasure is all mine."

She wrapped the sarong around her hips and tied a knot at her waist. "And who is this beautiful kitty?"

The cat soaked up the attention.

"This is Elliot," Drake explained.

She rubbed under the cat's neck. "Such a handsome fellow."

"What do you think of the island?" Drake asked.

"It's perfect. I couldn't imagine a place I'd rather be than here right now."

Neither could he.

Her cheeks and nose looked sun-kissed. She was so…lovely.

She sighed. "If I lived here, I doubt I'd ever want to leave."

"That's what I tell my son every time he packs up to fly to London," Rhys said. "The only thing that would make the island more perfect is a golf course."

Elliot jumped out of Drake's arms and chased a butterfly across the sand.

"Once the hurricane season is over, construction will start on your golf course."

Realization dawned on Chaney's pretty face. She stared up at Drake. "You own this island."

"Yes," he admitted. "My father lives here year round with Elliot. I stop by when I can."

"So the time you had cookies…?"

"Here."

"Is Elliot is your cat?" she asked Rhys.

"No," Rhys said. "But he tolerates me when Drake's away. Don't you, boy?"

She studied Drake with a questioning look in her eyes. "You have an island and a cat?"

"Yes."

"You're just full of surprises, Drake Llewelyn."

So was she. His gaze drifted lower. Chaney wearing a sarong was almost criminal.

He reminded himself she wasn't trying to torture him. She was here to do her job. Speaking of which… "How has the taping been going?"

"The crew was ready to go after their break. The island has so many photo opportunities for beauty shots we're ahead of schedule. That's why I could squeeze in a swim." She picked up her beach towel and held it in front of her chest. "We've been waiting for you to arrive so we can shoot a couple of stand-ups. Tomorrow we'll do the wraparounds and interviews and, of course, a spin in the personal submarine."

"Drake loves his toys," Rhys said.

"Most men do." She smiled at his father. "I bet even you."

Rhys's grin took years off his weathered and wrinkled face. "That I do."

The way she stood there in her wet swimsuit

and sarong with water beading on her smooth skin made her look like a model, but none of the models Drake had dated over the years could charm his father, make his cat purr like an idling engine and keep a production crew in check. His respect grew, as did his attraction.

"The house manager said a storm was forming in the Atlantic," Chaney said. "I wonder if we should try to tape a lead-in at sunset tonight. Just in case the weather changes."

If Drake kept thinking of her as anything other than his associate producer, he was going to cross a line he didn't want to cross. She deserved better from him. Too much was at stake especially during this trial period. "Taping a lead-in tonight is fine."

"Great."

Her smile pleased him. Seeing her happy made him happy.

"I'll head up to the main house and get things set up for the shot." She turned to Rhys. "Nice meeting you."

"You, too."

Chaney gave Elliot another pat and looked at Drake. "See you later."

With that she walked away, her sand-caked feet carrying her across the beach at a quick pace and up the path.

"Forget about her being your employee," Rhys said. "I say fire her and go for it."

"I can't do that, Dad."

Even if Drake might want to at the moment.

He couldn't.

He'd promised her a secure position. He couldn't go back on his word. No way would he disappoint Chaney after she'd been disappointed by so many others.

But most of all, Drake knew what would happen if she wasn't his employee. And the thought where that might lead made one thing as clear as the sea in front of him.

Drake might not want to be Chaney's boss, but he couldn't afford *not* to be.

Professional. Be professional.

The mantra had helped Chaney survive tonight's taping, but barely. Drake's island paradise made being professional difficult, and so did he.

The setting sun dropped lower into the horizon, painting the sky with a beautiful palette of reds, pinks and yellows. The perfect background for the wraparound shot they'd just finished taping and…romance.

No. Romance wasn't in the script. It couldn't be part of the shooting schedule. Or her life.

We can't forget that I will be your boss again.

Mustn't forget that.

But the way he'd stared at her on the beach earlier hadn't been very bosslike. His appreciative gaze had made her even more self-conscious than usual wearing a swimsuit. Especially after all the pints of ice cream she'd been eating lately. Standing in the water, wet and nearly naked, had made her think about what he'd said to her the other night.

You are perfect just the way you are.

Just thinking the words gave her a chill, the good kind. Pathetic. Chaney really did need to get a life.

At least she had a job. She sat at a table, picked up her clipboard and reviewed the script for tomorrow.

A red moving dot on the terrace below the deck where she sat captured her attention, but when she looked closer, it was gone.

She blinked.

Nothing there. Must be her eyes playing tricks on her.

The red circle appeared again, a dot of light moving around randomly. She wanted to know what it was.

With her clipboard in hand, she rose and descended the steps. Halfway down, she stopped.

Drake sat on the edge of a large hammock. He

wore a pair of khaki shorts, a plain white T-shirt and no shoes. In his right hand he held a laser pointer. A huge grin lit up his face while Elliot ran across the stone-tiled terrace trying to pounce on the rapidly moving pinpoint of red light.

"Go get the light, boy," Drake said. "Then you can have another treat."

Her breath caught in her throat.

She had never seen Drake look so relaxed and carefree.

Attraction ricocheted through Chaney, starting at her heart before pinging off her brain and toes and making U-turns.

He'd worn a casual outfit during the taping a short while ago, but those had still been a designer brand. She knew because the clothing he wore on the show was part of a product placement agreement. Maybe what he wore now was from a designer, too, but the outfit made him seem more approachable.

Not good.

Approachable was the last thing she wanted Drake, her boss, to be. She backed up the stairs carefully so he wouldn't notice her. She took another step. A creak splintered the quiet. Cringing, Chaney froze.

"Hello, there," he said.

Once again that deep voice of his made her

knees wobble. This was almost as embarrassing as his seeing her in her swimsuit. "Hi."

Drake waved the laser pen around for Elliot. "This is his favorite toy."

"He looks like he's enjoying himself. You, too."

Drake nodded. "Come down here."

She descended the rest of the way.

He patted the spot next to him. "This hammock is big enough for two."

No, it wasn't. She held her clipboard in front of her like a shield. "I don't mind standing."

"Suit yourself." The cat chased the light. "The idea of shooting the wraparound was brilliant. Even Milt was impressed, and that's not easy to do."

Chaney lowered the clipboard. "Thank you."

"You have an eye for what works on camera."

She stood stand taller. "It's challenging to figure out what will work and what won't. I like that."

"It shows." Drake flicked off the laser light. "Have you thought more about whether you want to continue working once the taping is completed?"

"I…"

Elliot meowed.

Drake reached into his pocket, pulled out a treat and tossed it to the cat.

"The trial period just started," she said.

"But you're enjoying the work."

"Yes," she admitted. "I appreciate this opportunity."

"I want you to stay on."

Since Saturday night Chaney had thought more about Drake as a man than Drake as a boss. She bit her lip to keep from saying something she might regret.

"Let me know what it will take. Money, stock options, vacation time, car allowance." He tossed Elliot another treat. "I'm open for negotiations when you're ready to discuss a permanent position."

"Don't you mean *if* I'm ready?"

Mischief lit his eyes, reminding her of a child with a secret he didn't want to share. But there was nothing childish about Drake. "I prefer 'when.'"

The cat trotted over and rubbed against her.

Chaney knelt down and petted its soft fur. The cat's loud purring sounded like a machine.

"He likes you," Drake said.

"Elliot likes anyone who rubs him."

"He doesn't go up to any of the crew like that, and they've been here longer than you.'

"Maybe they aren't cat people," she offered.

Elliot rolled on his back.

"He loves to have his tummy rubbed," Drake said.

"I can tell." She rubbed the cat's soft, round belly. "Have you had him long?"

"Since he was about four weeks old."

"That's not very old."

"I found him in a paper sack near a dumpster. He wouldn't stop meowing," he said. "He was a scrawny thing. Ugly, but I couldn't leave him there to die."

Her heart sighed at the thought of Drake saving a tiny Elliot. A man who'd been abandoned by his mother wouldn't want to leave a deserted kitten. "Of course you couldn't."

"He's a handsome chap now."

As if on cue, Elliot rose to all fours and made a running leap onto Drake's lap. The cat rubbed its head against his face.

Emotion clogged Chaney's throat. She swallowed. "Very handsome and very lucky to have a dad who loves him so much."

Drake winced. "I'm not his dad."

Could have fooled her. "My dad calls himself our dog's dad."

"That's because he's already a dad. Elliot is my first pet," Drake said. "We didn't have any when I was growing up. Not enough space or money."

She knew about his past, but after seeing how far he'd come and all he had now, that humble, poor beginning seemed impossible.

"But if I had kids…" his voice trailed off.

Hearing those words come from Drake's lips was huge. She remembered what he'd said about not having a family, yet his almost wistful tone yanked at her heartstrings. She took a step toward him. "What?"

He shook his head. "I don't know why I said that. I've never really considered kids."

Chaney was happy he'd said it now. "But if you had kids…"

"I'd want them to have pets."

She stared at Elliot. "A cat?"

"Cats, dogs, hamsters, ponies. Whatever they wanted."

She could believe it. He was generous and gave those he cared about whatever they wanted. "How would the children's mother react to this menagerie?"

Drake shifted on the hammock. He fed Elliot a treat from his pocket. "Hypothetically you mean."

"I don't see any children or ponies running around here."

"As long as she wasn't allergic to any animals, there shouldn't be a problem."

"You'll need to ask any woman you want to date that question straight away."

"Question?" he asked.

"If they are allergic to any animals."

He shifted in the hammock. "I don't know why we are discussing this. I don't have time for a family, so asking that question would never be necessary."

Except he already had a family. Rhys and Elliot. One Drake made time for and doted on. Chaney had the feeling it was only a matter of time before he realized he wanted more family, even a wife.

Hope filled her.

She pictured him with a child on his lap, a son with dark curly hair and dark soulful eyes. Her heart beat in double time. "It was only a hypothetical question."

He shrugged. "So are you allergic to animals?"

"No," she replied with a smile. "But hypothetically speaking, I have a strong aversion to snakes."

CHAPTER NINE

RAYS of tropical light streamed into Chaney's room. An early-morning breeze blew through the open windows. The white billowy curtains looked more like sails luffing in the wind than drapes.

Lying in bed, Chaney inhaled the salty air and glanced at her clock on the nightstand—5:28 a.m.

A long day of taping awaited her, but going back to sleep wouldn't be a good idea. Sleep led to dreams. She didn't want to dream about Drake again. Thinking about him nonstop was bad enough.

She'd thought that once she set to work on the island, things would be different, but if anything Drake was on her mind more than ever. Granted, she was forced to spend time with him. First during the taping at sunset and then at the delicious alfresco dinner by the pool with the crew and Rhys.

Eating, drinking and laughing while a steel drum band played hadn't felt anything like work, but Drake had treated her professionally and with respect, the way he treated the entire crew. He'd acted like their boss, yet there'd been more, an appreciation for not only what she did, but also who she was. She'd never received that from anyone else in her life, not even her parents.

Only Drake.

Chaney sighed.

Drake Llewelyn was so much more than she'd imagined he could be, and she'd imagined quite a lot with her crush five years ago. He might be a globetrotting, play-to-win billionaire who spoke about not wanting love or a family, but the generous things he did for others, how he went out of his way to help those around him, made Chaney look past his words to his deeds and the man he inside.

To the wonderful, strong, giving, caring man inside.

Affection bubbled up and overflowed from her heart.

She could imagine a life with him, a fulfilling, lovely life in London or here or really anywhere. As long as they were together. With Rhys. With Elliot. With…children. Drake had jolted her biological clock out of hibernation and into overdrive. Settling down didn't seem like such a far-off idea anymore.

If only she knew what to do about it, about him.…

Chaney tossed back the white duvet, crawled

out of bed and put on the thick, white terry-cloth robe she'd found hanging in her closet when she'd unpacked. She walked out to her balcony and stood at the railing.

The sun spilled its golden light into the ever-changing sky. The glasslike surface of the pool seemed to run right to the edge of a cliff and cascade over the rocks to the turquoise waters of the sea below.

A quick swim would clear her head. She had time. The taping wouldn't start for an hour and a half. She noticed someone entering at the pool area.

A man. She took a closer look. Drake.

He wore board shorts and nothing else. Awareness pulsed through her. The man had a killer body. Trim and fit with just the right amount of muscle definition.

A physique like that wasn't made from sitting behind a desk or attending social events. It took discipline and working out on a regular basis to have an athletic body like Drake's. She knew he worked hard when it came to his business, but his jet-setting ways and playboy reputation suggested a disciplined lifestyle didn't rank high on his list of virtues.

Elliot rubbed against his leg.

Drake placed the cat on one of the comfort-able-looking chaise lounges then walked to the edge of the pool. He dove in, barely making a splash. He swam a lap, did an underwater turn and swam another. Back and forth he continued across the pool.

The rhythm of his freestyle strokes mesmerized her.

"Good morning, Chaney," Rhys said from the balcony next to hers. "You're up early this morning."

"I was thinking about going for a swim," she explained, embarrassed she'd been caught staring at his son like a lovesick teenager or…a stalker. "But I don't want to bother Drake."

"He won't mind."

But she minded because her daydreams seemed all too real. She needed distance. Chaney shrugged.

"Be patient with him," Rhys said.

"I don't have to be patient with Drake. He's an easy boss to work for."

Rhys eyed her curiously. "I've worked for many bosses over the years and never once did I stand watching them swim."

Heat flooded her cheeks.

"I'm sorry." He smiled. "I didn't mean to embarrass you. I only met you yesterday, but I like you, Chaney. You care about Drake. That much is obvious to me. And I think you're what my son needs."

"He needs an associate producer."

Rhys's eyes softened. "Drake needs more than that, but he might not admit it since he's your boss."

Chaney stared at the man in the pool swimming laps as if he were training for the next Summer Olympics. "He's an excellent boss."

The words sounded lame. She cringed.

"I'm sure he is a very good boss," Rhys said. "He's better at giving than receiving."

She glanced at the older man. "I don't know what you mean."

"Think about it, and you will," he said. "Go take your swim. Before it's too late."

Chaney stiffened. Too late for what? Her and Drake? No, Rhys probably meant before she ran out of time due to today's taping schedule.

Still she quickly changed into her swimsuit, put her robe back on and followed the steps down the hill toward the pool. The plants, bursting in every shade of green imaginable, lined the serpentine path. Explosions of pink and red blossoms added bursts of color. The scents of flower and salt-water permeated the air.

At the pool, she petted Elliot.

The sound of the water being churned stopped.

"Good morning," Drake said.

"Hi." His wet hair formed dark curls all over her head. Water dripped down his cheekbones.

Gorgeous, yes, but he was so much more than a pretty face. He understood her. She wanted to understand him. "A beautiful morning for a swim."

He nodded. "Dive in."

Chaney usually used the stairs to get into pools, but she wanted to be strong and brave like him. An equal. "I will."

He'd already seen her in her swimsuit, but she was still embarrassed as she removed her robe. She placed it on one of the other chaise lounges.

All the while, she felt his gaze on her and forced herself not to cower. As she walked to the edge of the pool, she kept her head high. Chaney took a deep breath and dove into the crystal water.

Warm. Refreshing. Wet.

She swam to the opposite end and back again. Once she'd completed a lap, she stopped and pushed the wet hair back from her face.

Drake sat on the edge of the pool, his feet in the water, watching her with his dark, intense eyes. "Want to race?"

"I saw how fast you swim."

"I'll give you a head start."

"No, thanks," she said. "Slow and steady. That's my motto."

"Nothing wrong with that, but everyone needs to shake it up sometimes."

"I'm not a shaker-upper." She looked up so the sun could warm her face. "The truth is I don't like a lot of change."

"Everything changes."

"Yes, and every time there's a big change in my life I've lost something," she admitted. "I'm tired of losing."

His eyes softened. "I'll let you win."

She looked at him. "You would do that even though you like to win?"

Drake nodded. "If it would make you feel better."

Her heart bumped. "But if we already know the outcome, we don't need to race."

"How you get to the finish line can be just as fun."

"I don't know about that."

He slid off the edge into the water. "Come on."

They swam, side by side. Not exactly a heated race to the finish, but Drake never passed her even though she knew he could have easily overtaken her. They continued swimming laps, but she always touched the edge first.

Chaney lost count of the laps. She didn't know how long they'd swum, but her legs ached and so did her arms. She felt out of breath, but the physical activity cleared her mind. For that she was grateful and kept swimming.

Ouch. Her calf. A knot. She reached for the side of the pool and rubbed her leg.

Drake swam over to her. "You're faster than you think."

"You let me win."

"Only the first time," he said to her surprise. "We were pretty even the rest of the time. A good match."

His words filled her with pride. And hope.

The pain in her leg intensified. She winced.

Concern clouded his eyes. "What's wrong?"

"A leg cramp." She tried not to grimace as she flexed her foot against the wall of the pool to stretch out the muscle. "My left calf. A charley horse."

She gritted her teeth.

"Want some help," he offered.

The pain intensified. Her fingers gripped the edge of the pool. "Please."

He reached under the water and touched her leg gently. "Tell me where it hurts."

His fingers hit the spot. She squeezed her eyes closed. "There."

Drake increased the pressure of his hands. Slowly, with expert fingers, he massaged her calf. "Relax."

Easy for him to say. Harder for her to do. Especially when she was trying to remember if she'd shaved her legs yesterday.

"You're tensing up," he said.

Her knuckles turned white holding on to the edge of the pool. "It hurts."

"Let go. Sit on my knee."

Her brain short-circuited at the thought. "I…"

He peeled her fingers off the edge and floated her closer to him. The hair on his legs brushed her thighs. She sat on his bended knee. "Hold on to me."

Oh, boy. She really had no other choice in this position.

Chaney wrapped an arm around his shoulders. His skin was soft and wet. His muscles bunched underneath her hand. This was awkward, uncomfortable and, except for the pain, a complete turn-on.

He rubbed and kneaded. "If you relax, this will be much easier on you."

"I'm trying."

His hands worked their magic on her tight, aching muscle. Drake's face was right next to hers. If she turned just so…

No. She couldn't do that.

Chaney closed her eyes. She took a deep breath and exhaled slowly. It was either concentrate on her breathing or kiss him.

"Good," he encouraged.

"You're very good." Her eyelids flew open. Heat flooded her cheeks. "I mean, your hands."

"My hands are at your command."

If only she could command them— Her hormones shot into overdrive, so did her heart. "You can stop now."

He didn't. "I want to make sure it's all gone."

A few more minutes with his hands all over her leg, kneading, pressing and rubbing, and she'd be the one who was all gone. A warning shot straight to her heart. Too late. She wasn't falling for him. She'd fallen right into the deep end. Uh-oh.

"It's better now," she said. "Really."

He pulled his hands from her leg and she slid off his thigh and reached for the edge of the pool. "Thank you."

His gaze met hers. "Anytime."

And she knew he meant that. He would help her anytime. With anything. Others, like Gemma or the crew, too, if he could. But would he have come to their rescue in the pool and rubbed their legs? That didn't seem like boss behavior. Far from it actually.

Chaney thought about what Rhys had said about Drake.

He's better at giving than receiving.

"You're always helping everyone out," she said.

"I like helping the people who work for me. Loyalty and hard work should be rewarded."

"Yes, but you do more than a typical boss, like give leg massages."

"You needed it."

"True." But she wanted him to admit he saw her

differently from the other employees. "Would you have done that for someone else?"

"I do what I need to do," he answered. "Dragon Llewelyn has one of the lowest employee turnover rates in the industry." Pride laced his words. "It also has one of the highest rates of job satisfaction."

"I'm not saying what you do doesn't work, it's just you gave me a job, a costume, a night pretending to be my boyfriend, a leg massage. What are you getting out of helping me?"

"A hardworking associate producer," he said, not missing a beat."

"Is that all you want?"

"It's all I need."

She didn't want to accept that.

A bird sang from somewhere nearby, the cheerful song a stark contrast to the tension building between them.

"Who helps you out when you do need something?" she asked.

"I…" He furrowed his brow. "I don't need much help."

"Everyone needs help."

"I suppose if I need something outside of the office, I pay to have it done."

That was so sad, but exactly as she'd thought.

"I know." He brightened. "You helped be out

when you filled in for Gem and I could go on holiday with my father."

Chaney let go of the side of the pool and treaded water. "You paid me."

"I did."

And he was paying her now. She took a deep breath.

Down below them, the surf washed against the shore.

"Who helps you out?" Drake asked.

She rarely asked anyone for help, either. Not her parents because she didn't want to worry them. Not Simone or Tyler just because. Yet she was here because of helping Gemma. And…

"You," Chaney said. "You helped me out by offering me this job."

"Maybe we're more alike than we realized."

"Maybe we are." And maybe Rhys was right about Drake needing her. She wet her lips. "What if we promise to ask for help the next time we need it?"

He shrugged. "Okay."

"Promise me."

Drake studied her. "Are you always this… challenging?"

"No, you just bring it out for some reason," she admitted. "You didn't promise me."

He mantled his forearms on the side of the

pool and raised himself out of the water. "The chef has something special planned for breakfast this morning."

"You're changing the subject."

"I'm the boss." A wry grin curved his lips. "I can do what I want."

Drake needed someone who didn't work for him. Someone he couldn't buy with jobs and benefits and perks and "help." Someone who would help him out because they cared for him, not because he'd bought their loyalty.

The way he was trying to buy hers.

The realization weighted her down as if two cameras had been plopped onto her shoulders.

"Come with me," he said with an expectant gleam in his eyes.

And Chaney knew…

As long as she worked for Drake, she could never be more than his employee. She could never give him what he needed. And, she realized with a pang, he could never give her what she needed back.

Chaney stared up at him with longing and…love.

What was she going to do?

What was he going to do about Chaney?

Drake hiked along the path lined with thick ferns and lush trees. A series of nature trails wove their way through Dragon Island. Some led to secluded crescents of untouched white sand. Others led into the hilly interior of the island like the one he walked on now.

He forced himself not to look back at Chaney, who was followed by Tony, one of the cameramen. Drake had been thinking about her since this morning at the pool. Having her set on his thigh had been sweet torture. He wasn't sure how he'd survived. And now…

Drake wanted to touch her entire body the way he'd touched her leg. He missed the taste of her lips, the feel of her hair in his hands. But he wanted more than the physical.

She made him want to take as well as give. But taking from Chaney would hurt her. And if he came to depend on her, she could hurt him.

"Are we almost there?" Tony asked.

"It isn't much farther," Drake said.

Tony blew out a puff of air. "You said that an hour ago."

"Come on," Chaney teased. "The camera can't be that heavy."

"You want to carry it?" Tony asked.

"No, thanks," she replied.

"If I'd known it was such a trek, I might have opted for the boat tour with Jesse and sent Kyle with you instead."

"Trust me, you picked the right destination

today." Drake took a left where the trail forked. "This is one of my favorite spots on the island."

"What's it called?" Chaney asked.

"Lovers' Lagoon." He focused on what needed to be done with the taping, not what he wanted to do with her. "We've hosted a few weddings on the island, and this is where the newlyweds come after the reception to spend their wedding night."

"Quite a walk for a pair of newlyweds buzzed from champagne toasts and eager to get on with their honeymoon."

"There's a more direct way to reach the spot if you take a boat," he said.

"Now he tells us," Chaney quipped.

Drake glanced back at her in a pair of shorts, tank top and baseball cap. Her tanned skin gleamed with sweat. "I thought you two might want some interior beauty shots."

A soft smile graced her lips. His chest tightened.

"Thanks for the thought, Drake. You're right," Tony said. "But I'm going to have to send you the bill for my massage."

"You'll get one when we return to the house. It's already been arranged." Drake's gaze returned to Chaney. "You, too."

"You are the man," Tony shouted.

Drake laughed. "No more charley horses for my associate producer."

Chaney sighed, then mouthed a "thanks."

He'd get her to come around with all the perks he offered if she worked for him. That was how he would get her to accept a permanent job once the trial period was over.

She liked what he could do for her. She'd admitted that after her parents' party. She liked working for him. She'd said so. She also liked it when he'd kissed her, but he really couldn't give her any more of those if he wanted to keep things professional between them.

The trail crested a small incline then dropped into a tropical oasis with a waterfall-fed stone pool, a hot tub, two-person chaise lounge and a small but luxurious bungalow with thick wood beams, a vaulted roof line and long, flowing white curtains.

Chaney gasped. "Oh, my."

Tony sighed. "Wow."

The two stood with wide eyes and open mouths. The place usually had that reaction on people. It had on Drake.

"Welcome to Lovers' Lagoon." He pointed to the trail between two torchlights. "That path leads to a secluded beach where a boat can drop off or pick up."

Tony checked the lighting. "This is going to be a killer part of the episode."

"I told you the hike was worth it," Drake said.

"I'm sorry I complained."

Drake smiled. "No apology necessary, but I do have a boat meeting us at the beach so you won't have to walk back."

Tony flashed him a thumbs-up. "I'm going to see the bungalow."

The cameraman disappeared inside.

Chaney walked to the double chaise lounge that sat a few feet from the water and ran her fingertips over the overstuffed cushion. She looked at Drake. "The entire island is idyllic, but this place feels more pristine…special."

"This spot, back when it was undeveloped, convinced me to buy the island."

"Why did you buy the island?"

"Because I could." He laughed, then the amusement faded from his eyes. "My dad wanted to live in a warmer climate. I wanted a place I could go, a private place that was all mine, whenever I wanted it. To drop in and out as my schedule allowed.

"This island sure allows you to do that."

"My ultimate playground."

"Or sanctuary." Chaney stared at the water cascading down into the pool. She closed her eyes. "Listen."

He would rather watch her. The serene look on her face captivated him.

"This is so lovely," she said. "Relaxing."

Drake wasn't exactly relaxed at the moment, but the lovely view in front of him was worth it.

She opened her eyes. "What's it like at night here?"

"Peaceful." He smiled, remembering. "Except…"

"What?"

"The first time I wanted to spend the night here, I got lost," he admitted. "I must have taken a wrong turn and found myself wandering alone in the pitch-black. I finally made it, relieved and exhausted and in desperate need of a shower."

"You came here alone?"

"I don't bring people here."

Two lines formed above her nose, the way they did when she didn't understand something. "Why not?"

"As you said it's a special spot."

Drake didn't bring many dates to the island, but the ones he had, he hadn't brought here. He wanted to wait for the right moment with the right woman. His gaze met Chaney's. Someone who would understand how special this place was to him.

She smiled.

He smiled back.

And felt himself slipping away, into her eyes, into her heart, into her. Forget his world, he wanted to be a part of hers and follow her siren's call wherever it might lead him.

Tony exited the bungalow. "Well, I know where I want to honeymoon now."

Drake looked away from her, breaking the spell she had over him.

"You're engaged?" Chaney asked.

"Nope," Tony said. "I'm just saying. If I did get married."

She smiled. "Well, it's good to have goals."

Drake had goals, big ones that made a difference in this world and a tremendous amount of money. But Chaney with her pretty face, sharp mind and challenging questions was messing with his goals, keeping him preoccupied, distracted, unprofessional.

"Goals, right." Tony gathered his camera gear. "You going to honeymoon here someday, Drake?"

He had a wild impulse to ask Chaney what she thought about honeymooning here. Uh-oh. That wasn't good. In fact, it was extremely bad and needed to be remedied this instant. "No honeymooning here for me."

"Have someplace even better in mind?" Tony asked.

Drake felt Chaney's eyes on him, could feel her anticipation from ten feet away. Sticking her in the same sentence as honeymooning wasn't at all bosslike. He looked away. His feelings for her were more serious and substantial than he'd realized. He cared for her more than was reasonable, given the circumstances, and needed to put an end to it. For both their sakes. "I'm never getting married."

Chaney pressed her lips together.

Tony glanced his way. "A confirmed bachelor, huh?"

"What woman would have me?"

"Yeah." Tony laughed. "What kind of woman would want to marry a good-looking billionaire?"

"Exactly."

Tony walked into the bungalow with his camera.

"What do you mean by that?" Chaney asked.

"Well, if my mom didn't even want me…" Drake tried to sound lighthearted, as if it really didn't matter.

Chaney's sharp gaze pinned him. "You're afraid of letting anyone close."

He rolled his shoulders uncomfortably. "I just like to call the shots in my relationships."

"Even with me?"

"Especially with you." He smiled, trying to tease but not quite able to pull it off. "That's why I hired you."

Chaney had to quit.

Standing on the white sand of a secluded cove

with Drake and Tony, she watched a boat motor to shore.

As long as she worked for Drake, he would call all the shots and she would always be his underling. They couldn't have a relationship. Things would never be equal between them.

But could she do it?

She'd been playing it safe for years, her entire life really. But playing it safe hadn't gotten her what she wanted.

Her former fiancé had been a safe choice, but he hadn't been what she really wanted. She'd picked a safe job, only that hadn't turned out so well, either. Safe wasn't working for her.

So why not try something different?

Drake wasn't a safe choice. He was a dangerous one, actually.

She sneaked a peek at him standing tall and proud, his lips pressed together and his jaw set. So handsome. So strong. So giving.

She wanted to give him what he needed, what he deserved.

If he would have her…

Fear coated her mouth. Her insides trembled.

Chaney tried to push her doubt away.

The opportunity for something wonderful was right in front of her. All she had to do was muster her courage and take a risk, a gamble on a chance at happiness.

At love.

She took a breath. And another.

The captain of the boat cut the engine.

If she didn't take a chance now, she would regret if for the rest of her life. She knew that with pulse-pounding certainty.

Chaney straightened. "I think I'll hike back instead of take the boat."

Tony wiped his brow. "Are you crazy?"

Time would tell. She shrugged. "It's not every day a person has an island to themselves. I'm sure I can find my way back."

"I'll go with you," Drake said, as she knew he would.

"Have fun sweating your way back on the trail, kids." Tony walked to the boat with his camera gear. "I'll think of you while I'm enjoying my massage."

She waved and headed back up the trail to the lagoon. Drake followed her.

"I'm going to grab a couple of water bottles from the house," he said.

Chaney sat on the chaise lounge, staring at the water gushing down into the pool. A honeymoon here would be perfect.

Drake handed her a bottle.

"Thanks." She scooted over. "Have a seat."

The cushion sank from his weight. He twisted

open the cap on his water. She did the same and took a sip.

"I've been thinking about your proposal and the trial period we agreed to."

He took a swig from his water.

"Working on *The Billionaire's Playground* has been challenging, rewarding and fun. A really great experience."

"There are more great experiences ahead."

"I want more. A lot more."

His features relaxed. His mouth curved into a smile.

"But I don't want to work for Dragon Llewelyn."

There. She'd said it. Put it out there. Taken the risk. Now she would have to see if her gamble paid off. Chaney held her breath.

His smile disappeared. His eyes darkened. "I don't want to lose you."

Relief flooded her. Her heart felt buoyant like a helium-filled balloon. She'd thrown the dice and come up a winner. "You don't have to lose me."

"Tell me what it will take…"

A few dates would be nice. Dinner and a movie. A walk along the beach at sunset. Romantic images of the two of them swirled in her mind.

"…to keep you at Dragon Llewelyn," he continued. "Don't be shy. You're a valuable employee."

Her heart deflated. "I don't want to be an employee."

"Of course you do."

"I don't want to be your employee."

"I'm a good boss," he said. "I'll make it worth your while to stay. Name your price."

Her price. Chaney stared at him heartbroken. "You don't get it."

She wondered if he ever would. Probably not she realized with a pang. Drake could never give her what she really wanted, what she really needed, because he didn't know how to love people. He bought them instead.

"Get what?" he asked.

Emotion tightened her throat, made it difficult to breath.

"This was a test." Her voice cracked.

"And you passed it," he said. "I want to hire you."

"I passed because I was willing to take a risk."

"I have no idea what you are talking about."

He didn't, and that was what hurt so bad. "I'm not for sale."

"I'm not trying to buy you."

"Just call all the shots so you don't get hurt like your mother hurt you."

His jaw tensed. "Don't try and analyze something you know nothing about."

"I'm only going by what you said." Chaney

blinked, trying to stop the stinging in her eyes. "But it's true, I don't know you, not the way I thought I did. Or hoped I might."

"I can give you anything you want."

"You can't even see what you're doing." She sighed. "The high salaries, the wonderful benefits, all the out-of-this-world perks. I don't want them. I don't want the job. None of those things are as important to me as…you."

Confusion filled his eyes.

"You mean more to me than any job, Drake. That's why I don't want to work for you," she admitted. "If you're my boss nothing could ever happen between us. I thought if I quit, all the obstacles between us would disappear, but I see now I was wrong."

"Tell me what you want from me."

"Love, Drake. That's what I want."

"Love is overrated," he said. "It doesn't last."

"Says who?" She stood. Her bottle of water thudded against the ground. "I want to be loved, not bought. I want your heart, not things. I want you."

"I've given you everything you asked for, everything I have to give."

"It's not enough for me. I want…"

"More."

"I do want more from you. I deserve more."

His nostrils flared. "So when are you leaving?"

She hadn't said anything about leaving. "What?"

"If you no longer want the job, I'll need to make arrangements for your departure. And find someone else to fill in for Gem."

Arrangements. Replacements. Work.

A flash of pain ripped through Chaney. She might have been a valuable employee to him, but that was all she was. She'd talked about loving him, and he was more concerned with finding someone to take her place.

Her lungs seemed to stop working. She struggled to breathe.

He'd said she was perfect just the way she was, but he only wanted her if she would do as he asked. Just like every other person in her life....

Her heart withered, like a flower left out too long in the sun.

Tears welled in her eyes, but she wouldn't give him the satisfaction of seeing her cry. He wanted everything professional. Fine. She could do professional. And would.

"I said I'd be the associate producer for this final episode, and I will stay until the taping is completed." Chaney raised her chin. "As for my travel arrangements, I will leave when the crew leaves."

CHAPTER TEN

DRAKE stood next to one of the storm windows protecting his office from the driving rain and hurricane-force winds. "Butt out, Dad."

"I just asked what Chaney has been up to the last couple of days," Rhys said. "We haven't seen her much since the storm hit."

A palm frond blew across the deck and smashed into the house. The weather matched his mood.

His feelings for Chaney had only intensified, knowing she'd wanted him. Not seeing her, talking to her, touching her these past two days was driving him crazy. "I have no idea what she's been up to, okay?"

Rhys raised an eyebrow. "A little touchy are we?"

Damn. Drake grimaced. His dad was so playing him. All he'd had to do was keep his mouth shut, but instead he just let his father see how all this had been affecting him. "Chaney has decided to leave Dragon Llewelyn."

"Good for her."

He pressed his lips together in irritation. "Thanks a lot, Dad."

Rain pelted the windows.

"Now that Chaney's not working for you." Excitement filled Rhys's eyes. "You can make your move."

"I'm not making any moves on her." Chaney hadn't acted as a woman trying to manipulate a guy, but Drake wasn't about to give her what she wanted—a fantasy—only to have her walk out the door six months later. "You know women, they always leave you eventually."

"Not all women."

"Just the ones who count."

"Oh, son." Rhys shook his head. "Your mother, God rest her soul, didn't leave you. She left a bad marriage."

"The reasons don't matter. You said it was best to keep the past in the past."

"I was wrong." Regret filled his father's voice.

"Dad, you've always done your best."

"With you, not your mother." Rhys got a faraway look in his eyes. "When I met her, it was an exciting, wild time. I was older, but got caught up in the moment. We eloped without a thought to the future. Turns out she wasn't strong enough to deal with the life she'd married into, and I wasn't responsible enough to support a family. We were both at fault. Not just her."

"She's the one who left."

"Yes, except… You're too young to remember, but there was a time I didn't come home," Rhys said. "The only reason the marriage lasted as long as it did was because of you. I thought about trying to make a go of it again, but decided not to when she said she wanted to go home and start over with a clean slate. Your mother was better off with her family than me."

"We were her family."

"For a time, yes." Rhys gave him a warm smile. "But you, son, you are my family. All I have ever wanted, and that's why I never regretted loving or marrying your mother."

Elliot appeared from under the desk and brushed against Drake's leg.

"She was a beautiful woman, but your mother didn't know how to face challenges. Obstacles stopped her dead in her tracks," Rhys continued. "She wasn't the kind of woman Chaney is."

"You don't know Chaney all that well."

"No, but I know what you've told me," Rhys said. "And Chaney seems like a very special woman. I had something special with your mother for a time. I'd hate for you to lose your chance because you're too scared."

A pressure built in Drake's chest, threatening to explode. "I'm scared, right."

"It takes two people to screw things up, son. Just look at your mother and me," Rhys said. "And it takes two people to make things work."

"I tried to make it work with Chaney." She was the one walking away all in the name of...love. Drake set his jaw.

"Did you now?" Rhys asked.

Drake nodded. "She wasn't interested in what I was offering."

"Tell me what you offered her."

"A job."

"A job, you say?" Rhys chuckled, much to Drake's annoyance. "I hear that's a sure way to win a woman's heart."

He gritted his teeth. "I wasn't trying to win her heart."

"Then why are you so upset, stalking around here like a caged tiger ready to bite whoever comes near?"

Drake didn't—couldn't—answer.

"You know, son, you can always hire another associate producer." Rhys picked up a meowing Elliot. "Though finding one who looks as good as Chaney in a swimsuit may be a challenge."

The next day, patches of blue poked through the steely gray sky. The airport would reopen later tonight. Chaney and the rest of the crew could finally head home tomorrow.

But she didn't feel any relief packing her suitcase. No boyfriend. No job. No prospects.

Simone would be thrilled about this latest turn of events. Except, Chaney didn't really care what her sister thought anymore. She wondered why she had in the first place. What others thought of her didn't have anything to do with who she was.

Chaney folded a pair of shorts and placed them in the suitcase.

So what if she was in the exact same place she'd been two years ago when Tyler dumped her? This time was different. Back then she'd been more embarrassed than truly heartbroken because she hadn't really loved him. With Drake, she loved him. She'd taken the risk and lost, but she'd experienced love, real love.

Loving someone was a good thing even if it hurt. Loving Drake had shown Chaney want she wanted—what she needed—to be loved for who she was, not what she did.

Granted, she might not be ready to take another gamble on love again for a while, but she would. Chaney wasn't going to give up on the love she wanted. The love she deserved.

Somewhere there had to be a man who would

love her as she was and want to be loved by her in return. Not hide behind a fat bank account and dole out dollar bills and job perks as if they were kisses.

I've given you everything you asked for, everything I have to give.

Not everything. Not his heart.

Hers splintered more at the thought of Drake.

Chaney closed her suitcase and locked it. The rest of her items would fit in her carry-on bag.

Tomorrow would be a new day, a brand-new beginning. But tonight she had a party to attend. And she was going to enjoy herself at the wrap party. She'd earned it.

At Lovers' Lagoon, Drake cleared storm debris from the water. The physical labor felt good, what he needed after being cooped up in the house. The sweat running down his back reminded him of when he was a kid and did yard work for people to earn money.

He pulled a palm frond from the water and tossed it onto the ground. Chaney had stood right here a few days ago when she'd told she wanted more from him.

He skimmed the top of the water with a net, scooping out leaves.

More.

Chaney had attempted to dictate the terms of

their relationship by telling him what she wanted and what she would accept. She should have done that with her family in order to get the love she so desperately craved from—

I want to be loved, not bought. I want your heart, not things. I want you.

She wanted him. She wanted his love.

And he wanted…

Her.

Not as his associate producer. Not as his employee. Not as anything other than his love.

Love.

The realization was like an arrow to his heart. She'd spelled out her wants and her feelings, opening herself up to him, risking her heart and getting hurt. But he hadn't listened. He hadn't wanted to listen because her words, the emotions behind them, had made him…vulnerable.

Afraid.

Drake sat on a rock.

He'd spent his entire career, practically his whole life, taking risks to reap the rewards. But taking a risk on love…

The odds wouldn't be in his favor.

It takes two people to screw things up, son. And it takes two people to make things work.

Drake had never done that kind of work before. That kind of work didn't carry a guarantee of success or a material payoff. That kind of work wasn't about keeping score.

Except…

He stood and tossed the net onto the ground.

A future with Chaney would be the biggest reward of them all.

And that was what he wanted.

Her. Her love. Everything she had to give.

Stepping over branches and palm fronds, he made his way to the trail.

Chaney hadn't wanted to leave him. She'd wanted to stay with him. Not because of what he could do for her or give her, but because she loved him.

He'd just been too scared to accept it. Accept her.

No longer.

Drake would show Chaney he felt the same way and hope her feelings for him hadn't changed.

He would show her he could risk as much as she had. That he could be as brave as she'd been. That he could give her what she wanted. The fantasy. Even a happily ever after.

And he would.

Jogging down the trail, he dialed his father's cell phone.

Drake was just going to need a little help to pull it off.

* * *

"To the completion of yet another successful season." Milt raised his flute of champagne as a million stars twinkled and a half-moon lit the night sky. "May *The Billionaire's Playground* be our playground for many years to come."

Chaney raised her glass along with the rest of the crew. The one person missing from the wrap party was Drake. No one knew where he was. All Rhys had said was he had left the island, but would return later.

Later.

Just like that last night at the castle, but she knew her days of sharing cookies and milk and conversation with him were over. Chaney took a deep breath.

A gentle wind blew off the water. The flames of the surrounding torchlights danced. Hurricane glasses protected the lighted candles on the table.

She sipped the champagne, the bubbles tickling her nose. This time tomorrow she'd be back in Los Angeles. If not for the storm, she would be there right now. She would have already said goodbye to the crew, Rhys, Elliot and…Drake. Her stomach churned at the thought of leaving the island tomorrow.

Chaney was happy to be here with these people instead.

She glanced around the table at the faces she'd gotten to know so well over the past month. Staying awake during middle-of-the-night shots, trudging through lousy weather or terrain to reach the perfect location, putting out fires, both figurative and real ones, and having a really good time when the long hours were over for the day. She might not be happy how things turned out with Drake in her personal life, but professionally, she couldn't have asked for a better job.

"Thank you all for showing me the ropes," Chaney said, her throat dry. Even though she hadn't been part of the show long, the crew had accepted her and become her friends. "Taping four episodes with you guys taught me more about television than working two years in the finance department."

"They probably paid you better in finance," Tony joked.

"And didn't force you to wear low-cut, tight-fitting medieval gowns," Russell said.

"Or capture every minute of it on tape in hopes of a costume malfunction," Chaney teased.

Laughter filled the air. She joined in, but felt as if she were walking along a narrow edge, trying to balance the fun of the wrap party with her broken heart.

"I wish I could intern again next year." Jesse blinked back tears. "This is the best job ever."

The longing in the young woman's voice reminded Chaney of her own internship and going-away party five years ago. She'd walked away from that disillusioned, in a rush, eager to prove herself. This time she'd found herself and knew what she wanted. No more rushing. No more having to prove herself or anything else. She'd come full circle.

"Your internship is just the beginning of your career," she said. "And the first of many jobs."

Liz nodded. "Who knows, Jesse? You might come back to work here someday. Just like Chaney."

"That would be so wonderful." Jesse sighed. "I do hope I get to say goodbye to Mr. Llewelyn."

"Drake said he would be back. He will be," Milt said. "Though he'd better have one helluvan excuse for missing this party."

That seemed to appease the young intern.

Chaney wasn't sure what she wanted to say to Drake. *Thanks for the job, but it sucks you broke my heart and dashed my dreams again.* Perhaps a simple goodbye would suffice or, better yet, not a word. The thought of saying anything to him shattered her. Maybe it was better he wasn't here. She sipped from her water glass.

Cicadas chirped.

Another delicious-smelling course arrived at

the table, a medley of fresh seafood with a cream sauce, carried by the ever-amenable wait staff.

As people finished eating, Tony stood and readjusted a camera he'd set up by the table.

"Why do you have a camera out?" Chaney asked.

"Milt told me to get some tape of tonight. I think it's for the network or something."

"Maybe an extra if they put the show out on DVD," she offered.

"That could be it." He returned to his seat.

A different noise caught her attention. Not insects, something up in the sky. A helicopter.

Drake.

He'd returned. She closed her eyes, mustering courage and strength.

The sound of the rotors grew louder, drew closer. The helicopter disappeared over a hill on its approach to the helipad.

Jesse straightened in her chair. "That must be Mr. Llewelyn."

Milt nodded. "He'll be down here as soon as he can."

Raw and jagged pain sliced through Chaney at the thought of seeing Drake, of saying goodbye forever. But that was what she needed to do. The only thing she could do.

Tony returned to the camera. Another breeze rustled the palms.

She felt a hand on her shoulder and looked over.

"Maybe we could get together when we're back in L.A.," Liz suggested. "Go shopping. Have coffee. Try to meet some nice guys."

Chaney had enjoyed getting to know Liz at the tapings and could see them being friends outside of work. "I'd like that a lot."

Liz grinned. "I'll give you a call once we're home."

"Please do."

The breeze picked up, blowing through the fronds and bushes. A light floral fragrance hung on the air. The scent reminded Chaney of the flowers Drake had sent her.

Darn it.

She wanted to stop thinking about him.

Chaney heard the click of a speaker coming on. She glanced toward the sound and saw Rhys with a big smile on his face. Suddenly music played from speakers hidden somewhere. The melody sounded vaguely familiar.

Oh, no. Apprehension coursed through her. It was the song she and Drake had danced to at Gemma's Halloween party.

Chaney shifted in her seat. No big deal, she told herself.

"Isn't this a UB-40 song?" Kyle asked.

"Elvis sang it first," Milt said.

"Elvis Costello?" Jesse asked.

Milt shook his head. "Kids these days."

Chaney tried not to listen to the lyrics, but couldn't help herself. Grief tore at her heart. It was just a song, she reminded herself, and swallowed around the CD-size lump in her throat.

"Chaney," Drake said from somewhere behind her.

She turned in her chair.

He stood wearing a pair of khaki pants and a navy polo shirt. The tenderness in his eyes squeezed her already aching heart.

"They're playing our song." He extended his arm. "May I please have this dance?"

Every beat of her heart, every breath, hurt.

Frustration welled up inside of her. She wanted to dance with him. She still wanted him, even knowing he could never give her what she wanted.

"Go on," Liz urged. "It's not every day you get to dance with a billionaire."

The rest of the table encouraged Chaney, including Jesse, who motioned her forward with her hands.

Still Chaney hesitated, torn by conflicting emotions. None of the people egging her on knew the significance of this song. Only her and…

Drake.

She couldn't believe he was trying to hurt her on purpose.

"Please." His dark eyes implored her. "One dance."

Like their one kiss? Chaney couldn't help but be cynical.

Tony pulled out her chair. "Don't disappoint the boss."

The boss had already disappointed her. Still she rose from her chair and walked toward Drake, feeling utterly miserable.

She stood between his feet, placed one hand on his shoulder and the other in his hand. His familiar scent surrounded her, affecting her more than the champagne she'd drunk.

No armor separated them this time, only air and fabric. Much-too-thin fabric. As he took the first step, his thighs brushed against hers.

Chaney could barely breathe.

This was too much for her to handle. Her heart was breaking even more.

"I can't do this," she whispered.

"Yes, you can."

He led her around the deck, as smoothly and effortlessly as before, only this time her feet didn't cooperate. She kept stumbling and missing steps. He didn't let her clumsiness stop him. He continued dancing as if she were Ginger Rogers and he Fred Astaire.

Chaney tried to regain control, to pretend she

was dancing with someone else. She stared at the moon's reflection in the water. Anything to keep from looking at Drake.

Okay, this was a little better. She might actually get through the dance without falling or losing it.

"I should have listened closer to the lyrics of this song the first time we danced together," Drake whispered.

"Why is that?" she asked.

"Because in spite of all my efforts to the contrary, I can't help falling in love with you."

Chaney's gaze snapped to his.

"It's true." He stared into her eyes. "I love you, Chaney."

Her heart reeled. Those were the words she'd longed to hear from him. Only from him.

He loved her.

She had to be dreaming, a fairy tale of a dream with a handsome prince. If that was the case, she never wanted to wake up.

"You are the one who read my number," he said. "Who saw me, the real me, not just the billionaire seeking his next playground. You didn't want to be my employee. You wanted to be my equal, my partner, and that scared the hell out of me."

"You don't seem scared now."

"I'm terrified."

She recognized the vulnerable look in his eyes.

She'd felt that way herself. Time to take the leap. "Will it help if I say I love you, too?"

The relief flooding his eyes answered her.

"It's true," she admitted. "I love you, Drake."

A wide grin lit up his entire face. "I'm going to want to hear you say that over and over again."

"Is that an order?" she asked.

"A request," he said. "No more orders. I don't want to be your boss."

Tingles shot through her. "I can live with that."

"Good." He spun her around the deck. "You are the most amazing, intelligent, beautiful woman, Chaney. You don't let me do what's comfortable. I can't control you the way I do everyone else. You demand more from me and won't settle for what I can do or buy for you. And…"

She listened, tongue-tied but thrilled.

"It's exactly what I needed. Need." The love in his eyes brought a sigh to her heart. "You challenge me to be a better man. I'm sorry for letting you down, but I would be grateful for a second chance."

His words reassured her. Chaney forced herself to breathe. "A second chance sounds wonderful to me, but you have to know I let you down, too. You showed me what I needed. You made me want to be more and have more."

"There's nothing wrong with that, darling."

"Except I took all you had to give. It was all about me. We kept talking about quid pro quo except I didn't consider you or what you needed."

He ran his finger along the line of her jaw. "My father told me it takes two people to screw things up. And it takes two people to make things work. We'll both have to work at this."

"I'm game."

"Me, too."

The pitter-patter of her heart seemed to be singing a love song of its own.

"The only thing I need is you." Affection gleamed in Drake's eyes. "I need you in my life, Chaney. I'm willing to do whatever it takes to make it work. If you'll have me."

Her heart soared. "Love is always a gamble, but someone once told me you can't win if you don't play."

"I wonder what fool told you that," he teased.

"The fool who's ready to rush in."

"That would be me."

Laughter spilled out. "And me, too. I thought I needed everything laid out, all neat and tidy, before I could give my heart. But all I really need is to be loved, loved for who I am. No conditions, no qualifications, no expectations."

"Sounds good to me." He spun her around again. "I love you, Chaney Sullivan."

"I love you, Drake Llewelyn." Joy flowed through her. "Five years ago I had a crush on you, but even then I'd wanted you to be my Prince Charming. And now I know for certain you're my one true love."

"And you're mine."

He kissed her until her knees went weak.

Applause sounded. Chaney blushed. "I forgot we weren't alone."

"Me, too." Drake kept his attention focused on her. "But in a few minutes they'll be preoccupied if my father pulls off his second assignment for the evening."

"Your father?"

"You told me to ask for help the next time I needed it, so I asked him."

A satisfied feeling settled over her. "I saw him right before the music played."

"That was the first thing he had to do tonight," Drake said. "You'll have to wait for the second."

"No hints."

His smile crinkled the corners of his eyes. "It's a surprise, darling."

"Coming from you that could mean anything."

"You know me too well."

She touched his face. "And you me."

The song—their song—came to an end. The crew applauded once again. Milt and Tony didn't look surprised, but everyone else did. Surprised but happy.

Not as happy as Chaney, though. She felt as if she were floating and didn't care if her feet ever touched the ground again.

"I guess this means we'll have to postpone getting together, if you won't be heading back to L.A." Liz raised her glass to them. "And when we do get together, limit our outing to shopping and coffee since you seem to have found a nice guy already."

Chaney looked at Drake. They had said they loved each other, but she didn't know if that meant a long-distance relationship or what.

He had swept her off her feet. She knew she was taking a risk. Okay, the biggest gamble of her life, but she knew without a doubt this was the right thing—the only thing—to do. She was following her heart. Drake's love was enough for her. "Do you want me to stay here or go home or—"

"You are home." Drake knelt next to her, to the delighted gasps of their friends. "Five years ago, I asked you to stay with me. I don't blame you for saying no, given the offer I made, but I'm asking you again. Stay with me. Not as my employee, not as my girlfriend, but as my wife. I love you, and I don't want to let you go."

Chaney blinked. A tumble of emotions—shock,

joy, anticipation, love—ran through her. She forced herself to breathe.

He took her trembling hand. "Chaney Sullivan, will you marry me?"

She stared up at him through the tears of happiness in her eyes. "Yes, yes, I'll marry you."

The crew whooped, cheered and clapped.

"My heart is yours. Only yours." Drake pulled a diamond solitaire engagement ring from his pocket and placed it on her finger. "It always will be."

"And mine yours." She had found the kind of love she'd always dreamed of finding. A peace settled around her heart. "This ring. Is that why you left the island today?"

He nodded. "I wanted you to have the whole fairy tale."

She stared at the beautiful ring. "Thanks. It's stunning, but please know, as long as I have you, I'll have everything I ever need."

Something whooshed up into the air and exploded over the water. Colorful fireworks lit up the black sky.

The crew oohed and aahed.

"Surprise, Chaney," he whispered into her ear.

Life with Drake would always be full of risks. And surprises. She couldn't wait.

"Thank you." Chaney rose up on tiptoe and kissed him on the lips. "And your father, too."

Drake kissed her again, a slow kiss full of love, the joy of today and the promise of tomorrow.

Fireworks exploded.

She grinned. "You were that confident I'd say yes."

"Hopeful," he admitted, touching her dimple with his fingertip. "If you said no, I figured I might as well go down in flames for all to see."

"What happened to the man who prefers better odds?"

"He realized he could be safe and have everything in the world except what he really wanted, what he really needed—or he could risk it and have it all."

"You play to win."

"This time I won the biggest and the best prize of them all." He kissed the top of her head. "And one who isn't allergic to animals. Elliot is going to want a lot of siblings. Four-footed as well as two-footed ones. No snakes allowed."

"I love you, Drake." Her heart felt as if it might burst with happiness. "You're dragon, knight, beast and Prince Charming all rolled up into one."

"You claim not to be adventurous, but you're braver than me, my love."

"That's only because you made me want to be brave."

She noticed Tony taping the sky. "Now I see why you wanted a camera set up."

"It's part of the episode," Drake said. "And I already know the title."

She leaned into him, soaking up his strength, his warmth and his love. "What's that?"

Laughter lit the gold flecks in his eyes. "The Billionaire's Proposal."